**From the desk of Emerald Larson, owner and CEO of Emerald, Inc.**
**To:** My personal assistant, Luther Freemont
**Re:** My grandson Jake Garnier

Within a few days, my grandson Jake will be arriving in Louisville, Kentucky, and settling in at the Hickory Hills thoroughbred farm. During the search to find the Garnier siblings, my team of investigators discovered that Jake has a six-month-old daughter he knows nothing about. The baby's mother, Heather McGwire, manages the farm, and Jake is not going to be happy that we failed to immediately disclose that information. I expect you to intercept his calls until he works this out on his own. He's more like his father than any of my other grandsons, so this will be a true test for Jake. We'll see if he accepts the responsibilities of fatherhood, or runs from them the way his father did.

As always, keep me informed of the progress. And it goes without saying, I rely on your complete discretion in this matter.

Emerald Larson

Dear Reader,

We hope you enjoy *The Billionaire's Unexpected Heir,*
written by *USA TODAY* bestselling author Kathie DeNosky.

Every month in Harlequin Desire you'll find six new
powerful, passionate and provocative reads…guaranteed!
For more than twenty-five years, whether set on the French
Riviera or deep in the heart of Texas, Desire's highly
sensual romances have swept readers up in the tempestuous
drama of falling in love.

Go ahead…surrender to Desire!

Happy reading,

The Harlequin Desire Editors

P.S. Visit www.tryharlequin.com to download more than
16 free books and experience the variety of romances that
we publish!

# KATHIE DeNOSKY

# THE BILLIONAIRE'S UNEXPECTED HEIR

Recycling programs
for this product may
not exist in your area.

Copyright © 2011 by Harlequin Books S.A.

ISBN-13: 978-0-373-20277-5

The contents of this book may have been edited from their original
formats. The publisher acknowledges the copyright holders of the
individual works as follows:

THE BILLIONAIRE'S UNEXPECTED HEIR
Copyright © 2009 by Kathie DeNosky

Excerpt from ONE NIGHT, TWO HEIRS
Copyright © 2011 by Maureen Child

This edition published by arrangement with Harlequin Books S.A.

For questions and comments about the quality of this book please contact us
at Customer_eCare@Harlequin.ca.

® and TM are trademarks of Harlequin Books S.A., used under license.
Trademarks indicated with ® are registered in the United States Patent
and Trademark Office, the Canadian Trade Marks Office and in other
countries.

www.Harlequin.com

**Printed in U.S.A.**

## Books by Kathie DeNosky

Desire

\*The Illegitimate Heirs

---

## KATHIE DeNOSKY

lives in her native southern Illinois with her big, lovable Bernese mountain dog, Nemo. Highly sensual stories with a generous amount of humor, Kathie's books have appeared on both the *USA TODAY* and Waldenbooks bestseller lists and received a Write Touch Readers' Award and a National Readers' Choice Award. Kathie enjoys going to rodeos, traveling to research settings for her books and listening to country music. Visit her website at www.kathiedenosky.com.

This book is dedicated to Charlie, the love of my life.

And a special thank-you to my editor, Krista Stroever. Here's to new beginnings.

# One

"Hi, I'm Jake Garnier, the new owner of Hickory Hills."

From the corner of her eye, Heather McGwire saw the man stick out his hand in greeting, but she chose to ignore the gesture. She knew who he was and she'd just as soon have a snake crawl up beside her. Jake Garnier was the last person she wanted or needed to have to deal with this close to the big race. But now that he was the new owner of the thoroughbred farm she managed, there was no way of getting around it. She either had to get used to working for him or stick it out until after Stormy Dancer won the Southern Oaks Cup Classic, then look for employment elsewhere.

Besides, after what they'd shared, she took exception to the fact that he didn't even have the decency to remember her. The thought hurt more than she would have imagined or was comfortable with.

When she remained silent, he stared at her a moment as if trying to place her. "Heather?"

His smooth baritone caused her nerves to tingle and her heart to speed up, reminding her that a little over a year ago all it had taken was the rich sound of that voice to make her lose every ounce of sense she ever possessed. Now it only made her want to smack him for being the biggest jerk to ever draw a breath.

"Jake." She barely managed a short nod of acknowledgment.

Standing with her forearms resting on the white board-rail surrounding the practice track, she concentrated on the stopwatch in her hand as Dancer passed the quarter-mile post and headed down the backstretch. The top contender for the prestigious Southern Oaks Cup Classic, the thoroughbred was on pace to break his own record.

"Come on, Dancer. You can do it." She glanced from the watch to the horse. "Just keep it up."

"I remember you mentioning that you worked at a thoroughbred farm, but I wasn't aware that it was Hickory Hills," he said, sounding a lot happier to see her than she was to be seeing him.

"For the record, I'm the manager here." As Dancer

headed for the home stretch, she added, "The name of the farm and where it was located never came up. Besides, you weren't that interested in hearing personal details, were you?" She glanced his way, and it was apparent her hostility didn't set well with him.

"Heather, I don't know what you think I've done, but—"

"It doesn't matter now," she interrupted. She didn't care to be reminded of how foolish she'd been.

He was silent for a moment. "At the risk of pissing you off further, how have you been?" he asked tightly.

*Like you really want to know. If you had, you wouldn't have refused to take my phone calls.*

She shrugged. "I've been all right." She didn't bother asking how he'd been because she had a fair idea of what he'd been doing since they parted ways and didn't particularly care to hear the specifics.

"Is that our contender for the big race?" he asked, pointing toward Dancer.

Doing her best to ignore the man beside her, she urged the jockey, "Let him have his head, Miguel. Turn him loose." She glanced at the silver stopwatch again, and clicked the button on the side as the big bay sprinted past them. "Fantastic."

"I take it that was a good run?"

When Jake leaned close to see the time, his arm brushed hers and a tiny jolt of electricity shot straight through her. "It was excellent," she said, gritting her teeth and backing away. Turning to make her escape, she added, "Now, if you'll excuse me, I have work to do." She barely suppressed the urge to run when he fell into step beside her.

"I'd like for you to give me a tour of the farm if you have the time."

"I'm sure you need to unpack first," she said. Thanks to the mansion's housekeeper, Clara Buchanan, Heather had received a phone call the moment he passed through the security gates at the end of the half-mile-long driveway leading up to the mansion.

She desperately tried not to notice how his outstretched arms caused his snug hunter green T-shirt to outline the muscles of his broad chest and emphasize his well-developed biceps when he stretched. "I've been cooped up in the car for the past four days on the drive from Los Angeles and it feels good to be out in the fresh air again."

"Mornings around here are pretty busy—we have our daily workouts and grooming," she hedged.

When they reached the stables, she grabbed a lead rope by one of the stalls, slid the half-door back, then eased inside to attach it to Silver Bullet's halter in an effort to escape Jake's disturbing presence.

"All right," he said, stepping back as she led the big dappled gray gelding out of the stall and down to the tack room. "This afternoon will be soon enough."

She shook her head as she tied the rope to an eye hook by the tack room door, attached another rope to the halter, then tied it to another hook on the opposite wall of the wide stable aisle. "That won't work. My schedule is pretty full today and to tell you the truth, tomorrow isn't looking all that good."

"Clear it for this afternoon." Jake's no-nonsense tone indicated that he was quickly running out of patience.

For the first time since he walked up beside her at the practice track, Heather met his irritated blue gaze full-on with a heated one of her own. "Will there be anything else, Mr. Garnier?"

Scowling, he stared at her for several long moments before he finally shook his head. "I'll be back after lunch." Turning to leave, he added, "And you might as well plan on working late this evening. After you show me around, I intend to meet with the other employees, then I want to go over the accounting records."

As she watched him walk away, a nudge against her leg had her glancing down at the big Bernese mountain dog that had sidled up beside her. "You could really use some work on your guard dog skills, Nemo. Instead of taking a nap in my office, you're supposed to keep varmints like him away."

The dog didn't act the least bit repentant when he looked up at her adoringly and wagged his thick black tail.

Returning her attention to the matter at hand, she released a frustrated breath as she picked up a brush and began grooming the gray. She had no idea how he'd managed to get his hands on Hickory Hills, but she'd told herself when she learned Jake was the new owner that she'd be able to handle seeing him again. That she could keep what happened between them all those months ago separate from their working relationship.

Unfortunately, that was going to be a whole lot easier said than done. The sound of his voice carried with it the memory of him calling her name as they made love.

Closing her eyes, Heather rested her forehead against the big thoroughbred's shoulder. Over the past year she'd done everything she could to convince herself that Jake wasn't that good-looking, that her perception of their only night together had been clouded by loneliness and the haze of too much champagne. But she realized now that she'd been in deep denial.

Jake Garnier was well over six feet of pure male sex appeal and it was no wonder that he had an endless stream of women clamoring for his attention. With broad shoulders and narrow hips, he had the lean, muscular body of an athlete. When they'd met at the thoroughbred auction in Los Angeles, he'd been striking in a suit and tie, but today in jeans and a T-shirt, he was raw sensuality from his thick black hair to the soles of his outrageously expensive running shoes.

Sighing heavily, she went into the tack room, retrieved a saddle, then returned to place it on the horse's back. She tightened the saddle's girth, then bridling Silver, led him out of the stable toward the practice track.

As much as she'd like to forget what happened that night in L.A., she couldn't regret it. Jake was arguably the biggest player on the entire West Coast. But there was an earnestness to his charm that she'd found completely irresistible. And she was reminded of how captivating it was each and every time she gazed into her baby daughter's eyes. Eyes that were the same cobalt blue and held the same sparkle of mischief as Jake Garnier's.

Walking back up the path from the immaculately kept stables, Jake wondered what the hell had just taken place. He wasn't used to getting the cold shoulder from women and Heather's blatant snub didn't sit well.

There were only two things besides his siblings and highly successful law practice that caught and held his attention for any length of time and that was fast, flashy cars and shamelessly uninhibited women. And to his immense pleasure, the first frequently attracted plenty of the latter.

So why did one woman's obviously low opinion of him matter? He wasn't sure, but there had been a sparkle of hostility in Heather's eyes that had taken him completely by surprise.

Thinking back to the first time he'd seen her, he still couldn't believe how captivating she'd been. He'd attended a thoroughbred auction to personally see that the woman he'd represented in a bitter divorce sold the horses she and her husband had purchased as an investment. Jake had quickly lost interest in the parade of equine offerings and, looking around, had spotted a pretty little filly of the human variety to divert his attention. And from the moment he introduced himself to her, he found Heather to be the most enchanting woman he'd ever had the pleasure of meeting.

They'd spent the rest of that day and one incredibly sensuous night together and over the course of the past year he'd come to the conclusion that he should have asked for her last name and a number where he could reach her. It was totally out of character for him and something he'd never contemplated before. Once he parted ways with a woman, he never looked back, never had the slightest regret about not contacting her again. At least he hadn't until Heather.

But surely she wasn't angry that he hadn't kept in touch over the fifteen months since. Besides the fact that he didn't know how to reach her, it was a well-known fact that he wasn't looking for a relationship of any kind and that none of his liaisons went any further than a good time.

He had no idea if that's what the problem was, but he had every intention of finding out and settling the animosity between them once and for all. If she was going to be running the horse farm that his newfound grandmother, Emerald Larson, had insisted he take over, it was essential that they get whatever had her panties in a twist straightened out so they could at least be civil.

In the meantime, he needed to unpack and put in a call to Emerald, Inc. headquarters to find out what the hell Emerald had up her sleeve this time. Given her track record of setting her grandchildren up to find their soul mate, he wasn't naive enough to think that she wasn't attempting to do the same thing with him. He wasn't sure how she'd done it, but she had to have discovered that, however brief it had been, that he and Heather had a bit of history.

But the old girl was in for a big disappointment if she thought her tactics were going to work with him. He wasn't looking to settle down with a wife, kids and the requisite canine. Nor was he inclined to trade his sleek little red Ferrari for a family-friendly minivan with car seats and clumps of dog hair.

With a plan of action to set down a few ground rules for both Emerald and his farm manager, Jake followed the path around the antebellum mansion to the circular drive in front where he'd parked his sports car. Just as he pressed the remote on his key-chain to open the trunk, a teenage boy wearing stylishly ragged jeans, an oversize chartreuse T-shirt with It Is What It Is screen-printed on the front and a red baseball cap turned backward on his head came out of the house to greet him.

"Hi, Mr. Garnier," the kid said, crossing the veranda and bounding down the steps. He came to a sliding halt at the side of the car, then stood staring at it as if in awe. "Suh-weet."

"Thanks," Jake said, chuckling at the way the boy stretched the simple word into two syllables. "And you are?"

"Daily." He grinned. "My dad was a horse trainer before he died and talked my mom into naming me after the Daily Double at Churchill Downs." He reverently circled the car. "Dude, I have *got* to get me a ride like this when I get old."

Jake realized that the kid was talking to himself and meant no disrespect. But the comment reminded him that within a few short weeks he'd mark his thirty-seventh year and he supposed that in the eyes of a young teenager, he was probably considered a fossil.

Smiling, Jake reached into the trunk for the suitcase he'd packed for his short stay at Hickory Hills. But Daily jumped forward to grab the handle.

"I'm sorry, Mr. Garnier. I didn't mean to get so carried away looking at your car." He hoisted the suitcase out of the trunk. "My grandma sent me out to get your luggage and take it upstairs for you."

"You're Mrs. Buchanan's grandson?" Jake asked, following Daily up the steps of the veranda.

The boy nodded. "Grandma's in charge of the house and Heather is in charge of everything else." Daily's youthful face suddenly split into a wide grin. "Wait until you meet Heather. For an older chick, she's way hot. Having her to look at every morning makes my chore of mucking out stalls a lot easier."

When Emerald and her stoic assistant, Luther Freemont, had met with him to turn over ownership of the farm, they'd informed him that Clara Buchanan was the live-in housekeeper. But they hadn't said a word about Heather being the farm manager. That just reinforced Jake's theory that Emerald was definitely up to something. Why else would she mention the name of the housekeeper and leave out all reference to the woman who ran the majority of the farm?

"I've met Heather." The kid couldn't be more than fourteen or fifteen years old, but it seemed he already had an appreciative eye for the ladies. "And I agree. She's very pretty."

When Daily opened the double doors and stood back, Jake entered the foyer and immediately felt as if he'd taken a step back in time. Decorated with furniture he had no doubt were period antiques, he half expected to see a woman in a wide hoop skirt descend the sweeping circular staircase. Or more likely a Kentucky colonel dressed in a white suit and holding a mint julep come strolling out of the study.

"Grandma told me to take your luggage up to the west wing," Daily said, walking toward the stairs. "If you want me to, I can show you where your room is, Mr. Garnier."

"Lead the way." When they reached the top of the staircase, Jake grinned. "I'll bet sliding down a banister like this one is as close to being on a roller coaster as you get without going to an amusement park."

"Oh, dude, talk about a rush," Daily said, his voice enthusiastic. He stopped suddenly, a concerned expression crossing his youthful face. "Uh, you probably don't want me doing that because of scratching the finish."

"It's water under the bridge now." Jake shook his head. "But I'm not as concerned with a few marks on the wood as I am about you taking a fall. That's a long way down and you could be badly injured."

"You won't tell my grandma, will you? She'll kill me if she finds out."

Jake took pity on the kid. "As long as you don't do it again, I think we can keep it between the two of us."

Clearly relieved to hear Jake would be keeping his secret, the boy smiled. "Thanks. You're really cool, Mr. Garnier."

"I'll take that as a compliment." Every time Daily

called him Mr. Garnier, he felt as old as dirt. "And while you're at it, why don't you call me Jake?"

After a delicious lunch, Jake strolled back down the path leading to the stables and couldn't help but wonder if he'd lost his touch with the opposite sex. He'd never had this much trouble with women in his entire life. If things didn't change, he just might end up developing a complex.

Emerald, for one, was purposely avoiding him and unless he missed his guess, she'd continue to do so for a while. She had to know he was on to her latest matchmaking scheme and no doubt wanted to avoid having him tell her to mind her own damned business.

But Mrs. Buchanan's sudden disappearance right after serving him lunch was a complete mystery. She'd been friendly enough when he first walked into the kitchen. But as soon as she put his plate in front of him, she'd apologized and rushed off to the housekeeper's quarters as if she thought he was contagious.

And then there was the chilly reception he'd received from Heather that morning. Her body language and obvious contempt let him know in no uncertain terms exactly how she felt about his reappearance in her life. But try as he might, he couldn't figure out why. He hoped for better luck with her during their meeting this afternoon, but he wasn't fool enough to count on that happening.

Entering the stable, he walked past several stalls to the opposite end of the structure where the manager's office was located. He wasn't the least bit surprised that Heather was nowhere in sight. Given her attitude toward him, he really expected no less. He wasn't, however, prepared for the very large, black dog that got up from a blanket in the corner, walked over and stretched out on top of his feet.

"At least you're friendly," he said, reaching down to pet the dog's head.

Irritated that she'd obviously blown off his request to set up a meeting with the farm employees, he extricated his feet from beneath the animal and covered the short distance to where the brood mares were kept. He found Heather bent over a horse lying on its side in one of the stalls, and his mouth went completely dry. She was dressed in a pair of faded blue jeans and a pale pink T-shirt. With the denim hugging her shapely little bottom to perfection, he didn't think twice about taking in the delightful view.

As she straightened, an older man Jake assumed to be one of the grooms brushed past him to enter the stall and hand her a pair of rubber gloves. When she pulled them on they extended up to her shoulders.

"What's going on?" he asked, venturing farther into the enclosure.

"The stork is going to make it before the vet."

She knelt down behind the horse in the middle of the oversize stall. "Jake, I want you to hold her head to keep her from trying to get up, while Tony and I take care of things on this end," she instructed.

Jake wasn't used to anyone issuing him orders, but something in Heather's tone had him kneeling down to carry out the directive. As he watched, the man she'd called Tony held the horse's tail, while she helped guide the foal from the mare. She quickly lifted a membrane away from the colt's nose, then vigorously massaged the animal's small, wet body with a towel.

"Is that to make sure it starts breathing?" He found her skill and efficiency to be very impressive.

Nodding, she pulled off the gloves and stood up. "He was doing pretty good on his own, but it never hurts to have a little insurance when it comes to foals this valuable." She smiled down at the weak little creature. "We may be looking at the next Triple Crown winner."

Rising to his feet, he moved away from the mare's head as she started to get her legs under her. "Do you have to do this sort of thing very often?"

Before she could answer his question the cell phone clipped to the waistband of her jeans rang, and she stepped out of the stall to take the call.

Jake turned to the groom. "By the way, I'm Jake Garnier, the new owner here."

Grinning, the man nodded. "I figured as much. Welcome to Hickory Hills."

"I have to go up to the main house for a few minutes," Heather interrupted, stepping back into the stall. "If you have any questions about the broodmares, training schedules or the farm's daily routine, Tony can fill you in."

Jake walked over to stand beside her. "I think I'll go with you, then you can show me around."

"There's really no need." Her long golden-brown ponytail swayed back and forth as she shook her head. "I'll only be a few minutes and there's no sense in you walking all that way just to turn around and walk back."

Had that been a hint of panic he'd detected in her soft voice? Why didn't she want him going with her?

"I don't mind at all," he said, placing his hand to the small of her back to usher her along. There was no way she'd leave him behind now. "Afraid of a little exercise?"

Jake could tell she wanted to protest at his wisecrack, but clamping her lips together, she quickly stepped away from his touch and preceded him out of the stall. Neither spoke as they walked side-by-side up the path to the back entrance of the mansion and he couldn't help but wonder what she was trying to keep from him. And he had no doubt there was something. He hadn't been an attorney for the past twelve years without learning to recognize when someone was trying to conceal a secret.

When they entered the kitchen, Jake stopped short at the sight of Clara Buchanan with a crying baby in her arms. Never in a million years would he have thought the emergency calling Heather away from work would be a baby. But his astonishment was compounded tenfold when Heather hurried over to them and took the child from the housekeeper. The baby instantly calmed down and it was obvious that Heather was the child's mother.

"I think she might be running a little bit of a fever," Clara said, touching the baby's round little cheek.

Heather nodded. "I thought she felt warm when I got her up this morning." She tenderly pressed her lips to her daughter's forehead. "I think she might be trying to cut her first tooth."

"That's what the pediatrician said when I called her." The housekeeper smiled fondly at the tiny girl. "But I wanted to let you know and see what you thought about taking Mandy in to her office."

"It might not be a bad idea to have a doctor check her over," Jake said from behind her.

He knew even less about babies than he did about horses. But he and his twin brother, Luke, had raised their ten-year-old sister after their mother was killed in a car accident and remembered that when a child had an elevated temperature it was always better to err on the side of caution.

"Just to be on the safe side, I think I will take her to see Dr. Evans."

"I'll get the diaper bag," Clara said, disappearing down the hall toward her apartment.

As she and Jake stood in uncomfortable silence while she waited for Clara to return, Heather felt as if her nerves had been stretched to the breaking point. Was Jake aware that he was standing barely four feet away from his own daughter? Had he noticed that Mandy had his blue eyes and dark hair?

Ever since she'd learned that he was taking over Hickory Hills, she'd wondered how she was going to break the news to him about the baby. But she hadn't anticipated him meeting their daughter before she had a chance to tell him about her.

He hadn't said anything. Maybe he hadn't noticed how much Mandy looked like him. If that was the case, she'd be able to explain everything in a much less rushed fashion. She hoped.

"Needless to say, I won't be giving you that tour of the farm this afternoon or holding the meeting you wanted with your employees," she finally said as she cradled the baby close.

He nodded. "That's understandable. We can reschedule for tomorrow morning or even the day after if she's still not feeling well."

When the housekeeper came back into the room, he reached out and took the diaper bag from her. "I'll help Heather and the baby get to the car."

"Call me when you get back to let me know what you find out from the doctor about our little angel," Clara called after them as they left the house.

"Would you mind letting Tony know that he's in charge until I get back?" Heather asked as they walked the short distance to the carriage house.

Jake shook his head as he watched her open the back door of the older-model sedan parked in front. "No problem. I'll take care of it. Is there anything else?"

"Not that I can think of."

When Heather turned to put the baby in the car seat, the little girl looked at him over her mother's shoulder for the first time and he felt as if he'd been flattened by a steamroller. He couldn't have gotten his vocal cords to work if his life depended on it and simply stood back as Heather got into the car and drove away.

As he watched the vehicle disappear around the corner of the mansion and head down the drive toward the main road, his heart pounded against his ribs and he found it extremely hard to draw air into his lungs. The baby had dark hair and big blue eyes. Eyes the color of cobalt. The same color of cobalt that met his gaze when he looked into the mirror each morning to shave.

# Two

That evening, when Heather answered the insistent knocking on her cottage door, she wasn't the least bit surprised to find Jake standing on the other side. In fact, she'd been expecting him. She'd known that once he saw Mandy it was just a matter of time before he put it all together.

"We need to talk." Instead of waiting for her to invite him in, he took hold of her elbow and propelled her back into the living room, kicking the door shut behind him. "I want answers and I'm not leaving here until I get them, Heather."

"It never crossed my mind that you would," she said calmly. She wasn't going to allow him to upset or stress her out in any way.

"That baby belongs to me, doesn't she?" he demanded, cutting right to the heart of the matter.

"*That baby* has a name—Amanda Grace. I call her Mandy. She's almost seven months old." Heather walked across the room to pull the nursery door closed to keep their raised voices from disturbing her daughter. "And if by belong, you mean are you her biological father? The answer is yes."

"What happened? I used protection."

Was he actually questioning that he was the father of her child?

"I'm well aware of that. It obviously had a defect." She raised an eyebrow. "Surely you're aware that nothing is one hundred percent effective except abstention. And if we'd gone that route—"

"We wouldn't be having this conversation," he finished for her.

"Exactly." She looked him directly in the eye. "But let me assure you, Mandy is your daughter."

He shook his head. "I wasn't questioning that. She looks just like me."

Heather watched a muscle work along his lean jaw as Jake stared at her for what seemed like an eternity. She could tell his anger was bordering on outrage, but that was just too bad. As far she was concerned, not knowing he'd fathered a child was his own fault and she wasn't about to let him turn the blame back on her.

"Did you even think about getting in touch with

me when you discovered you were pregnant?" he finally asked, his voice low and menacing.

Heather had told herself that she wasn't going to let him get to her, but his accusatory tone angered her as little else could. "I really don't think you want to go there, Jake. Believe me, you won't like hearing what I have to say."

"Go ahead. Try me." He took a step toward her. "I told you I'm here to get answers."

"Then I would suggest you drop the intimidation tactics as well as the idea of being the wounded party in all of this because you're not." When she turned to walk into the kitchen to put a little more distance between them and the nursery, she fully expected him to follow.

He didn't disappoint her. "Did you or did you not consider letting me know that you were expecting my child?"

Turning on him, she took a deep breath in an effort to calm down. She had a lot to say and she was going to savor every second of it. She'd wanted this conversation for over a year, but never thought she'd have the chance to have her say. She wasn't going to allow herself to lose momentum by becoming overly emotional. She refused to give Jake that kind of power over her.

"I not only considered letting you know, I spent my first trimester leaving messages that I needed to talk to you urgently." She met his angry gaze head-on.

"*You* never returned my calls, and I wasn't comfortable leaving that kind of information with your secretary."

"I—"

Holding up her hand to stop whatever lame excuse he came up with, she went on, "Then I spent the second trimester trying to convince myself that there had to be a reasonable explanation for you ignoring my requests to get back to me. It turns out I was wrong. There wasn't a good reason, other than you really are an insensitive, self-absorbed jerk who uses women, then casts them aside."

He opened his mouth to no doubt refute her assessment of his character, but she cut him off again.

"And somewhere during the course of my third trimester, I came to the conclusion that you really didn't deserve to know about our daughter and that we were both going to be a lot better off without you in our lives." She folded her arms beneath her breasts. "Any more questions?"

Heather could tell by the stunned look replacing the angry expression on his handsome face that she'd gotten through to him.

Rubbing the back of his neck as if to relieve tension, he shook his head. "I have my secretary—"

"Screen your calls so that you don't have to deal with uncomfortable situations with the women you've bedded," she interrupted. When he remained silent, she knew that her comment had hit a little too close to home. "And you don't have to worry, Jake. Mandy and I are just fine on our own."

His eyes narrowed. "You're going to try to cut me out of her life?"

Heather shook her head. "That's not what I said. I'm telling you that you're off the hook. You're free to go back to Los Angeles and resume your life as if nothing happened. I don't want or need your help—financially or otherwise. I'm perfectly capable of taking care of and providing for my daughter. I just thought you had the right to know about her."

"She's mine, too."

Having had her say, she suddenly felt drained of energy. "I'm relieving you of that responsibility, Jake."

"I think we need to get this straight once and for all, Heather."

He stepped forward to place his hands on her shoulders. The heat from his touch seeping through her T-shirt and the determination she detected in his deep baritone sent tingles zinging straight up her spine. But when he used his thumb and forefinger to lift her chin until their gazes locked, the sensation danced across every nerve in her body.

"I accept that it was my own damned fault I didn't know about the pregnancy. But it doesn't mean that now that I'm aware I have a child I don't intend to be a big part of her life. And that will be much easier for me to do when I move you and Mandy into the mansion with me."

"That's not going to happen, Jake. We're very happy right here in the carriage house."

"We'll see about that."

Before she could protest or step away, his mouth covered hers and the feel of his firm lips once again caressing hers with such care caused her head to spin. She tried with all of her might to remain unaffected, but her traitorous pulse took off and a delicious warmth began to flow through her veins.

Placing her hands on Jake's wide chest, instead of pushing away from him as she intended, she reveled in the feel of his strength beneath her palms and the steady beat of his heart. This was total insanity. He'd used her, then cast her aside with little or no regard for her feelings. But when he traced the seam of her mouth with his tongue, she parted her lips without so much as a second thought and allowed him to deepen the kiss.

As he wrapped his arms around her and pulled her more fully against his large frame, he teased her with a tenderness that caused every fiber in her being to quiver to life and her stomach to flutter wildly. The excitement she'd experienced in his arms fifteen long months ago began to fill her from head to toe and it scared her as little else could. Losing herself to Jake's kiss was the very reason they found themselves in their current set of circumstances.

"Please...stop," she said, leaning away from him.

Jake immediately put a bit of space between them, but continued to hold her loosely in his arms. "All things considered, I probably shouldn't have done that." He gave her the same seductive smile that had been her downfall that night in Los Angeles. "But I'll be damned if I'm sorry I did. You have the sweetest lips I've ever tasted."

She shook her head. "Forget my lips. It's not going to happen again."

He stared down at her for endless seconds and just when she thought he was going to argue the point, Nemo chose that moment to come lumbering in through the doggie door. Finding the two humans standing face-to-face, he apparently took it as an open invitation to push his way between them and plop his big, bulky body on top of their feet.

"What's his deal?" Jake asked, staring down at the dog. "Every time he sees me, he traps my feet beneath him."

Thankful for the distraction Heather stepped back then knelt down to scratch the big gentle dog behind his floppy ears. "It seems to be a trait of his breed. I think they realize that they're too big to sit on your lap, so they lay on your feet to be close to you."

Jake bent down to pet Nemo's thick, black coat. "So I guess this means he likes me, huh?"

"It looks that way." Only inches apart, they stared at each other for endless seconds before she straightened to walk back into the living room to peek inside the nursery.

She should have named the dog Benedict Arnold. Nemo was supposed to be loyal to her, not cozy up to the enemy like they were long-lost friends.

"What did the pediatrician say this afternoon?" Jake asked from behind her shoulder. "Is she cutting her first tooth or is something else wrong?"

Unaware that he'd followed her, Heather jumped as much from the unexpected sound of his voice as from his close proximity. "Uh...yes, she's teething. The doctor said she has two that should be through her lower gum by the end of the week."

"She'll start feeling better after that happens, right?"

Heather nodded as she pulled the door closed and moved away from him. The concern in his voice touched her and that was something she didn't like one bit. It was much safer for her to think of him as the shallow, uncaring man who refused to take her phone calls, than a daddy worried about the welfare of his baby girl.

"I think it would be a good idea if you leave now, Jake." She walked over to open the front door. "I have to be up by five in the morning and I really need to get some sleep."

Glancing at the gold watch on his left wrist, he nodded. "I have a lot to do tomorrow and need to be up early myself."

He walked over to her, then cupping her cheeks with both hands lightly pressed a kiss to her lips. As he raised his head, the determination she saw in his incredible blue eyes sent a shock wave all the way to her soul.

"If you and the baby need me before morning, don't hesitate to give me a call. You have my word that from this day forward, no matter what I'm doing or where I am, I'll always be available for you and our daughter."

Once the front door closed behind him, Heather squeezed her eyes shut against the tears of frustration threatening to spill down her cheeks. She'd known the former owner was looking to sell, but why did Jake Garnier have to be the new owner of Hickory Hills? What cruel quirk of fate had caused their paths to cross again? And why, after all that had happened, did she still find him to be the most handsome, irresistible man she'd ever met?

When he'd introduced himself at the annual thoroughbred auction in Los Angeles, he'd not only charmed his way past her defenses and swept her off her feet, he'd stolen her heart, as well. She'd always heard about love at first sight, but she'd never given it a lot of thought, never believed it would happen to her. Not until last year. Not until Jake.

Swallowing hard, she reminded herself of the disillusionment and emotional pain she'd suffered when he refused to return her calls and she'd realized she meant absolutely nothing to him. It had taken her a long time to move past that and no matter how drugging his kisses were or how wonderful it had felt to be in his arms, she wasn't about to put herself in that position again.

Besides, it wasn't just her emotions at stake anymore. She had Mandy's well-being to take into consideration, as well. And Heather wasn't going to stand back and watch her daughter bond with Jake, then be devastated when he moved on like the playboy he was.

As he walked down the long driveway toward the big wrought-iron entrance gates, Jake still couldn't quite wrap his mind around everything that had happened. In the span of a few hours, his life had changed in ways he could have never imagined. He had reconnected with the only woman he'd ever regretted not keeping in touch with, learned that by taking over Hickory Hills she'd become his employee and discovered that a little over six months ago she'd given birth to his baby.

Unbelievable.

But as he thought about Heather making several attempts to get in touch with him, his gut burned with anger. He deeply regretted that she'd been forced to go through the pregnancy alone. If his secretary hadn't become overly zealous about screening his calls, she wouldn't have. He'd have not only been there for Heather throughout the pregnancy and birth, he wouldn't have been cheated out of the first six months of his daughter's life.

His daughter.

Jake's heart slammed against his rib cage and he took several deep breaths. He had a tiny baby girl who looked just like him.

It blew his mind that he had a child. Fatherhood had been something he'd never expected to experience. And it wasn't because he didn't like little kids. He did. He'd just made a conscious decision years ago never to marry and have one of his own.

His own father had twice walked away after impregnating his mother, and even though Jake didn't think he was capable of doing something like that, he hadn't wanted to take the chance. What if he carried the same narcissistic gene that had caused his father to shirk his responsibilities to his children in favor of pursuing his next good time?

Jake shook his head. It was all a moot point now. He had a daughter. And even though it scared the living hell out of him to think that he might somehow let her down the way his father had his children, Jake was going to do everything he possibly could to be a good father.

Lost in his disturbing introspection, it took a moment for Jake to notice the shadowy figure climbing over the gates at the end of the drive. "Daily?"

The boy froze halfway over the gate. "Mr. Garnier,

I…oh, dude, this probably doesn't look real good, does it?"

"No. It looks like I just busted you for sneaking out of the house." Stopping a few feet from where the boy was perched, Jake planted his feet and folded his arms across his chest. "You want to come down from there and tell me why you're out this late, as well as why you don't want to alert anyone up at the house that you're leaving by activating the gates?"

When Daily dropped to his feet in front of Jake, he seemed to take a great interest in the tops of his untied high-top tennis shoes. "It's kind of personal, Mr. Garnier."

Jake hid a smile. "Want to tell me what her name is?"

The boy's head snapped up so fast, Jake wouldn't have been surprised if Daily had suffered whiplash. "How did you know I was going to meet a girl?"

Jake did his best not to laugh out loud at the astonished look on the kid's face. "I know it's probably hard to believe, but I was fourteen once, Daily."

"I'll be fifteen in a couple of weeks," the boy said, straightening his skinny shoulders.

"That's still too young to be out this late. Not to mention the fact that you don't have your grandmother's permission."

The boy's shoulders slumped. "Yes, sir."

"I think you'd better give your girlfriend a call

and tell her that you won't be able to make it this evening," Jake suggested.

As he watched Daily whip out a cell phone and rapidly punch in a text message, a knot began to form in the pit of Jake's stomach. In about thirteen years some pubescent boy with more hormones than good sense could very easily try to set up a midnight meeting with his daughter.

He barely managed to suppress a groan. He'd already raised one girl through the teen years when he and his twin brother finished raising their younger sister, Arielle. And just thinking that he was going to have to do it all over again with his own daughter was enough to give him an ulcer. His only consolation was that this time he'd be sharing that responsibility with Heather, instead of his brother who had turned out to be as clueless as he'd been.

When the boy slipped his cell phone back into his jeans pocket, Jake motioned toward the tree-lined drive leading up to the mansion. "Come on, Daily. I think it's time we both called it a night."

They remained silent for some time before Daily asked, "Are you going to tell my grandma about me trying to sneak out tonight?"

Jake shook his head. "No, I'm not. But you are."

"Me?"

"Part of growing up is learning to accept responsibility for your actions," Jake said, reminding himself as much as Daily.

"I'm gonna be grounded for the rest of my life," the boy complained when they entered the mansion through the kitchen door.

"I doubt it will be that long," Jake said, chuckling. "But as long as you're going to be sticking close to home for the next week or so, there are a few things around here I'm going to need help with. Do you think you'd be interested in the job?"

"A real job? Really? Oh man, that would be awesome," Daily said, his voice suddenly filled with enthusiasm.

"You'll have to keep up with your other chores and check with your grandmother first, to make sure she has no objections." Jake gave the boy a pointed look. "Right after you tell her about what happened this evening and accept whatever punishment she deems necessary."

Daily nodded. "I will."

"Then you'd better get some sleep," Jake warned. "We have a big day ahead of us."

"Yes, sir."

As he watched the teenager hurry down the hall to his grandmother's apartment, Jake headed for the stairs. He'd made Heather a promise and he fully intended to keep it. While she oversaw Stormy Dancer's morning workout and attended to whatever else her job entailed, he and Daily were going to get her and the baby moved from the carriage house into the mansion. And once he accomplished that, he had every intention of spending the rest of his stay at Hickory Hills getting to know his daughter.

"Jake Garnier, how dare you?" Heather demanded when she found him sitting at the desk in the study. She was angry enough to bite nails in two and it was all his fault.

His unrepentant grin when he looked up made her want to throw something at him. "I assume you're referring to the moving of the baby's things and yours from the carriage house to the rooms upstairs?"

"You know good and well that's what I'm talking about. You had no right to do that."

He walked around the side of the desk to stand in front of her. "I don't know why you're so upset," he said calmly. "I told you last night that's what I intended to do."

She couldn't believe his arrogance. "And I told you it wasn't going to happen. Mandy and I are perfectly fine in the carriage house. It's all she's ever known."

"I'm sure you're happy." He took another step toward her. "But you'll be even happier here. There's a lot more room. And besides, it will be more convenient for all concerned."

"You've got to be joking." Where did he come up with that idea? "It might be more convenient for you, but it certainly isn't for me."

He was a lot closer than she was comfortable with.

But there was no way she was going to back away. That would only give him the satisfaction of knowing he still had an effect on her.

"I fully intend to be a big part of my daughter's life," he said, sounding so darned reasonable it made her want to punch him.

"We live less than a hundred feet away. How is moving to the big house going to change anything?"

He gave her a smile that caused her heart to skip a beat. Just because he smiled at her it wasn't going to get him off the hook.

"I want to watch you put her to bed at night and get her up in the morning."

"You could do that at the carriage house."

"So you're telling me that you want me to move in with you and Mandy?" he asked, giving her that same charming smile.

"N-no. That wasn't what I said at all and you know it." She should have known he'd twist her objections around to suit his purpose. After all, he was an attorney. "You knew what I meant. You could stop by around those times, then leave."

He took the last step separating them, then lightly touched her cheek. She suddenly had to remember why she was angry with him.

"If Mandy wakes up in the middle of the night, I want to be able to get up with her." He shook his head.

"If I'm here and the two of you are in the carriage house, I can't do that."

"Take my word for it, being awakened from a sound sleep is highly overrated," she said before she could stop herself.

"I'm sure that taking care of her by yourself and trying to work has been very tiring at times. Wouldn't it be nice for a change to have someone sharing that responsibility?"

When he looked at her the way he was doing now, Heather was lucky to remember her own name, let alone what he'd asked. "No. I'm fine with the way things are."

"I could get up with her while you sleep," he pressed.

The heat from his touch branded her and the scent of his aftershave made her want him to hold her, kiss her and… She swallowed hard. She needed to escape his presence before her traitorous body had her agreeing to go along with what he wanted.

"I—I don't mind at all being solely responsible for Mandy," she insisted.

"But you don't have to be, honey. Not anymore." He moved his hands down to her waist, then pulled her into his arms. "I'm here now and you don't have to do everything alone."

"Please, Jake," she interrupted. "Don't." Pulling from his arms, she somehow found the strength to back away from him. "I won't try to stop you from being part of Mandy's life. But I want you to keep a couple of things in mind before you take that step. First and foremost, it's all or nothing. You're either her father for life or not at all. I don't want her becoming attached to you, then you walk away when you get tired of playing daddy. And second, count me out. I'm not part of the package."

He stared at her for several long moments before he slowly shook his head. "You have my word that I will never do anything that isn't in her best interest or yours."

"Good. Because hurt my daughter and you'll have me to deal with." She could tell from his expression that he meant what he said—now. The only problem was, whether they intended to or not, people sometimes broke their promises and others ended up getting hurt.

"Now that we have your main concern out in the open and settled, are you and the baby going to stay here in the mansion?" he asked, seating himself back behind the desk.

"Jake, I don't think—"

"I've missed out on a lot with her already, Heather." His chest rose and fell as he took a deep breath. "All I'm asking is that you give me a chance to get to know my daughter and build a relationship with her."

She knew if she and the baby did stay in the mansion with him, she would be taking a huge risk for both Mandy and herself. If she hadn't known that before he kissed her last night, she did now. No matter how much he'd hurt her or how hard she tried to resist his charm, she still found Jake to be six feet two inches of pure temptation. And that could very well prove to be disastrous for her if she didn't keep her wits about her.

But she'd told him she wouldn't stop him from trying to bond with Mandy and she couldn't, in good conscience, deny either of them the right to get acquainted. And while he was getting to know their daughter, she intended to learn more about him, his family and where he grew up. After all, she had the right to know about her daughter's father.

Heather sighed heavily. Unfortunately, now wasn't the time to put him through the third degree. Aside from the fact that she'd already put in a grueling day, she was still too angry. She wanted to be calm, rational and in complete control when she talked to him.

"We'll stay in the mansion as long as you're here at Hickory Hills. But only on one condition."

His eyes narrowed ever so slightly before he asked, "And what would that be?"

Walking to the door, she turned back. "I meant what I said about not being part of the equation, Jake. Don't count on me to be one of your…diversions when you get bored."

# Three

Jake frowned as he watched Heather place their sleeping daughter into the small baby bed that he and Daily had set up earlier in the day. "Is that thing full size? It looks awfully small."

When she placed her finger to her lips, it was all he could do not to groan. He couldn't forget the kiss they'd shared the night before and wanted to once again taste her sweetness and feel the softness of her perfect mouth beneath his own. But he knew better than to push. She'd outlined her conditions and he had to admit it was probably for the best. It wouldn't be long before they had to address some very sensitive issues concerning shared custody and how they were going to raise Mandy. If they became involved, it could make doing that a lot more difficult. He just wished that the attraction between them wasn't as powerful now as it had been when they first met. That would certainly make things a lot easier.

"It's a mini crib," she whispered, drawing his attention back to his question.

He waited until she turned on the baby monitor, clipped one of the receivers to her belt and they'd both stepped out into the hall before he asked, "Why didn't you get a regular-size bed for her?"

"The room I turned into the nursery at the carriage house is small and I wanted to save space," she answered as they started downstairs.

"What about when she gets a little older?" he asked, following her. He didn't like the idea of his child being in a room that was too small when she had every right to live in the mansion and enjoy the spaciousness of any one of the spare bedrooms. "How will you fit a regular-size bed into that room and still have enough space for her to play?"

"When the time comes, I'll convert the room I use for a study into another bedroom." At the bottom of the steps, she turned to face him. "Why are you asking about this now? It won't be an issue for another year or two."

He smiled as the germ of an idea took root. "I was thinking that the two of you could live here in the mansion even after I go back to L.A."

"No. That's not an option," she said, shaking her head until her ponytail swayed back and forth.

"Why not?"

She started toward the hall leading to the kitchen. "Because it's not *my* home."

Reaching out, he took hold of her arm and the feel of her soft skin beneath his palm sent heat straight to the pit of his belly. He did his best to ignore it. "This is my house now and Mandy is my daughter. She has every right to live here."

Heather gave him a look that stated in no uncertain terms that she didn't like his idea one damned bit. "But it's not mine, Jake."

He knew as surely as he knew his own name that there was a good deal of pride holding her back from accepting his offer. "I'm telling you it can be, Heather."

"I work for you and living in the carriage house is part of my contract."

"I'm offering you an amendment to that agreement." Barely resisting the urge to pull her into his arms, he hastened to add, "You don't have to make a decision about the move being permanent now. But I would like for you to give it some serious thought." Unable to stop himself, he reached up to brush a wayward strand of hair from her soft cheek. "It would make life for you and Mandy a lot more comfortable than being cooped up in a space where there's barely room for one."

Before she could come up with any more excuses why she and Mandy shouldn't live in the mansion permanently, he reluctantly dropped his hand to his side and crossed the foyer to enter the study. If he hadn't put some distance between them, there had been a very real possibility that he would have acted on his first impulse to grab her and kiss her until she agreed to his proposal. And that would have been a huge mistake.

It would take a fool not to see that just like a magnetic force, the attraction between them was too strong to fight and impossible to resist. But at this point, she didn't trust him any more than she would a snake coiled to make a strike. And until he proved himself to her and they worked out an agreement to raise their daughter, he had no other choice but to bide his time and no doubt end up taking more than his share of cold showers.

He sighed heavily as he lowered himself into the chair behind the desk and reached for the phone. As he punched in his brother's number, he thought about the irony of it all. The only woman he hadn't been able to forget was back in his life, was the mother of his only child and thought him lower than the stuff she scraped off her boots after a trip through the stables.

"My life is just about as freaking wonderful as it can get right now," he muttered sourly.

"As a matter of fact, mine is going pretty good, as well," Luke said, laughing.

Wallowing in his own misery, Jake had missed hearing his brother answer the phone. "Good to hear, bro. How are things in Nashville?"

"We couldn't be better. Haley has passed the point where morning sickness is an issue and we're just waiting for the sonogram to see if we're having a boy or a girl." His twin sounded happier than Jake could ever remember.

"Glad to hear my favorite sister-in-law is feeling better," he said, wondering if Heather had experienced a lot of problems with morning sickness when she'd been pregnant with Mandy.

They were both silent a moment before Luke asked, "So what's wrong, Jake?"

"What makes you think there's a problem?"

He wasn't surprised by his brother's intuitiveness. As with many twins, he and Luke shared a sixth sense where the other was concerned and instinctively knew when things weren't going right. But Jake wasn't entirely certain how to deliver the news that upon his arrival at Hickory Hills he'd discovered he had a daughter and avoid having to listen to the I-told-you-so speech that was sure to follow. Luke had been warning him for years that his "love 'em and leave 'em" ways were going to catch up to him one day.

"You're talking to the only person who knows

you better than you probably know yourself." Luke paused. "So you want to tell me what's going on?"

"I have a daughter." Jake hadn't meant to deliver the news quite so bluntly, but once the words were out, he realized there wasn't any easier way to say it.

"Whoa! You want to back up and say that again?"

"You heard me," Jake said, wanting to reach through the phone and throttle his twin. "I have a six-and-a-half-month-old daughter named Mandy."

His brother was silent for so long, Jake wasn't sure they hadn't lost the connection. "And you found this out when you moved to the horse farm Emerald gave you?" Luke finally asked.

"Yeah." He took a deep breath. "Heather's the manager here at Hickory Hills. I'm betting when the old girl's investigators found us, they discovered that a woman I met at a Thoroughbred auction last year had become pregnant from our one night together."

"That explains why you ended up in a place about as far removed from your life in Los Angeles as it's possible to get," Luke agreed. "Arielle and I wondered why you were given an enterprise that was totally out of your element when we were given businesses in our respective career fields."

"I don't know why Emerald didn't just tell me about Heather and Mandy instead of blindsiding me like this," Jake complained. "Didn't she think I would step up and do the right thing?"

His brother made a strangled sound. "You're getting married?"

It was Jake's turn to choke. "Hell, no. You know how I feel about marriage. It's not for me."

"Don't knock it until you've tried it," Luke advised. "I didn't think I was husband material, either, and look at me now."

"Whatever."

They were silent a moment before Luke asked, "Why didn't the baby's mother tell you about the pregnancy?"

"She tried, but my secretary didn't see fit to give me the messages." Jake made a mental note to call the woman the first thing in the morning and discuss her not bothering to give him a list of callers.

"Ah, if you'll remember, I told you—"

"Don't say it, bro."

Luke's laughter grated on Jake's nerves. "So when do we get to meet our niece and her mother?"

"That's the reason I called. How would you and Haley like to come up to Louisville for the Southern Oaks Cup Classic in a couple of weeks? The favorite to win the race came along with the farm."

"Sounds good," Luke said. "I assume you're inviting Arielle and Zach?"

"Of course, along with the rest of the clan."

A few months ago, when he and his siblings

learned that the most successful woman in the corporate jungle was their paternal grandmother, they'd also been informed that they had three half brothers. After meeting them at one of Emerald's receptions and finding themselves in the unique position of being the unexpected heirs of one of the world's richest women, they'd become friends.

"And before you ask, I fully intend to invite our illustrious grandmother and her stiff-as-a-board assistant, too. She and I are going to have a little talk about her withholding information about my daughter," he added.

Luke snorted. "Good luck with that."

Making plans to talk again before the impromptu family reunion, Jake hung up, then called his other siblings to invite them to the gathering. With promises from all to attend, he walked into the foyer and ran right into Heather.

"Are you all right?" he asked, placing both hands on her waist to keep her from falling. A jolt of electric current as strong as a lightning strike shot through him and when she looked up, the awareness he detected in her aqua eyes let him know that she'd felt it, too.

"I—I'm fine."

"I'm sorry, I didn't see you," he said, filling his senses with her. The scent of her herbal shampoo and the feel of her softness beneath his hands sent heat coursing straight to the region south of his belt and his body's reaction was not only predictable, it was inevitable.

"I…was just…on my way upstairs." She sounded delightfully breathless and sent his blood pressure up a good ten points or so.

As if an invisible force held them captive they remained silent for so long, Jake finally forced himself to speak. "I…uh, was on my way to take a shower and call it an evening myself."

Still operating on West Coast time, he hadn't even entertained the idea of calling it a night. But he did need a shower. A cold one.

She nodded. "Well…I guess I'll see you in the morning."

"What time does Mandy wake up?" he asked, still holding her at the waist.

"Early."

Finally forcing himself to step back, he motioned toward the staircase. "Then it would probably be a good idea if we call it a night."

As if awakening from a trance, she blushed suddenly and, ducking her head, started walking toward the steps. "Good night, Jake."

"Night."

He stood in the foyer long after Heather reached the second floor and disappeared down the hall. The sound of her voice and the realization that she would be sleeping just down the hall from him had him fully aroused in less than a heartbeat.

Taking the stairs two at a time, he made a beeline for the master bathroom. By the time he reached his bedroom, he'd already stripped off his shirt and left a trail of clothing on his way to the shower.

As he stood there punishing his body beneath the frigid spray, he couldn't help but wonder how long Heather was going to deny the chemistry that flowed between them. They could fight it, try to run from it and argue that it even existed, but it was just a matter of time before they made love again. He had no doubt about that. The only question was when.

With a record-breaking crop of goose bumps and his teeth chattering like the windup ones found in a novelty store, he turned off the water. He grabbed a thick towel and began to vigorously dry off. They were going to have to work out the agreement for Mandy, and Heather had to come to her senses and accept the inevitable. He didn't particularly like shivering his ass off in a shower so cold he could spit ice cubes.

"Heather, I'm sorry, but I'm not going to be able to watch Mandy for you this afternoon. I forgot that I have an appointment with the high school counselor to get Daily enrolled and set up his freshman schedule."

"I suppose I could take her with me," Heather said slowly, wondering how she was going to attend a meeting at Churchill Downs with a baby in tow.

"We can change that to another day, Grandma," Daily offered, sounding hopeful. "I don't care. I'm not all that into school anyway."

"Young man, you'd better get 'into it' real fast," Clara said sternly. "You're in enough hot water as it is after that stunt you pulled the other night."

"Listen to your grandmother, Daily. If you want a car like mine when you get 'old,' you're going to need a good job. And that takes education."

"Yes, sir," Daily answered, shoveling a fork full of scrambled eggs into his mouth.

Looking up, Heather's heart skipped a beat as she watched Jake stroll into the kitchen and seat himself at the head of the table. Dressed in a light blue polo shirt that emphasized the width of his broad shoulders and a pair of jeans that hugged his muscular thighs like a glove, he wasn't just his usual good-looking self. This morning, he was white-hot. Busying herself with Mandy's breakfast, she tried her best not to stare.

"What time is the meeting?" Clara asked. "Maybe we'll be back before you have to leave."

Heather shook her head. "It's a luncheon meeting and probably won't be over until late afternoon." She spooned a bit of baby cereal into Mandy's eager mouth. "I'll just take her with me and hope she has a good long nap during the speeches."

"I can watch her," Jake spoke up as he took a

couple of strips of bacon from the platter in the center of the table.

"That's okay. I'm sure you have better things to do." She wasn't at all comfortable leaving her daughter with a man who she was almost positive had zero experience babysitting an infant.

Smiling, he shook his head as he took a sip of his coffee. "I don't have anything going on this afternoon. Besides, it will give Mandy and me a chance to get acquainted."

"Really, it's not a problem," she said firmly. "I'll take her with me."

An ominous silence suddenly reigned throughout the kitchen as Jake put down his coffee cup and their gazes locked. "Don't be ridiculous, Heather. She's my daughter, too. I have every right to watch her while you're busy."

"No way!" Daily said, his eyes wide. "You're Mandy's dad? I didn't know that."

"Come on, young man," Clara said, removing the boy's plate from the table. "You can finish your breakfast in our apartment before you go down to the stables to muck out the stalls."

"But, Grandma—"

"You heard me," the housekeeper said, cutting him off. "These two need to talk and they don't need you hanging on their every word. Now move."

Heather waited until Clara and a reluctant Daily left the kitchen before she turned her full attention back to Jake. "How many babies have you taken care of?"

"None."

"That's what I thought." When Mandy protested loudly, Heather spooned another bite of cereal into her mouth. "You don't have the slightest idea what to do with a baby."

His frown deepened. "I've got to start somewhere."

"My daughter isn't an experiment."

"She's *our* daughter." He placed his hand on top of hers. "I know you're worried I won't know what to do. But I promise, I'd never let anything hurt her."

She could tell from the sincerity in his voice and the look in his eyes that he meant every word he said. But he admittedly had zero experience with babies.

"I won't let her out of my sight the entire time you're away," he promised.

"Jake, I'm not at all comfortable with—"

"I'll even stay in the same room with her while she takes her nap," he interrupted.

"Have you ever changed a diaper?"

"No, but it can't be that hard to figure out. Besides, I'm a quick study," he said confidently. "You can show me how to put a new one on her before you leave."

She barely managed to hide a smile at his misguided self-assurance. He had no way of knowing that their daughter thought diaper changes were great fun and the perfect time to exercise her legs by kicking like a little karate champion.

"What about lunch?" she asked, beginning to realize she didn't have any other option. She couldn't get out of the meeting and it was no place for a baby. "Do you think you'll be able to feed her?"

"I watched you feed her breakfast and it didn't look all that difficult." He grinned. "Piece of cake."

Spooning the last bit of cereal into her daughter's mouth, Heather wiped the baby's face. "You'll call me if you have even the slightest problem?"

"Of course."

She lifted Mandy from the high chair and handed her to him. "Would you mind holding her while I wipe off the high chair and put it away?"

Jake had been too busy yesterday with the unauthorized moving of her things from the guesthouse to do more than watch her or Clara with the baby. It was time that father and daughter met officially. Besides, she needed to see how Jake was with Mandy before she agreed to him watching the baby.

He gently lifted Mandy to sit on his arm. "Hey there, Honey Bunny. I'm your daddy."

As Heather watched, the baby gazed at him intently for several seconds, then giggling, happily slapped her tiny hand against his cheek. But it was the look of awe and complete wonder that instantly came over Jake's handsome face that had her blinking back a wave of tears.

She wouldn't have believed it was possible to actually see it happen. But right before her eyes, Jake fell hopelessly in love with their daughter.

# Four

When Heather returned from her meeting, she practically burst through the back door of the mansion. She'd tried several times on her drive from the Downs to call Jake on her cell phone, but he hadn't answered and with each passing second her concern increased. Searching the rooms downstairs, her heart began to pound hard against her ribs when she couldn't find either of them. Why had she let him talk her into allowing him to watch her baby?

But her anxiety turned to mind-numbing fear when she hurried up the staircase and entered the bedroom where Jake had set up the crib. The two were nowhere in sight.

In a near panic, she raced down the hall to the

master suite. "If he's let something happen, I'll never forgive…"

Her voice trailed off as she came to a skidding halt just inside the suite door and a knee-weakening relief washed over her. There in the middle of the king-size bed her daughter lay curled up on top of Jake. Both were out like a couple of lights.

Leaning against the door facing, her panic began to recede and as she stood there catching her breath, she couldn't help but be touched by the moment. Heather knew for certain she'd never forget the poignant sight of her tiny baby girl sleeping so trustingly on her daddy's wide bare chest. For the second time in a matter of a few hours, she found herself blinking back tears.

Quietly, so as not to disturb either of them, she gently lifted Mandy into her arms and, walking back to the bedroom where the crib was, placed the baby in the small bed. Turning on the monitor, she clipped the receiving unit to the waistband of her khakis and turning to leave, came face-to-face with a wild-eyed Jake.

"Dear God, Heather, why didn't you wake me up to let me know you were taking Mandy?" he demanded. "When I opened my eyes and she wasn't there, I—"

Heather placed her index finger to his lips to silence him when the baby moved restlessly and let out a little whimper. "I'm sorry," she mouthed. She motioned for him to follow her out into the hall. "You looked like you might be a little tired from babysitting and I thought I'd—"

"Give me a heart attack," he finished for her.

That's when she realized that he'd been as terrified as she had when she'd been unable to find them. "I really am sorry. I didn't mean to frighten you."

Running a frustrated hand through his thick black hair, he took a deep breath. "I've never been that scared in my entire life."

As they stood there, she couldn't help but stare at his bare chest. Every muscle was well-defined and as her gaze drifted lower, she had an almost uncontrollable urge to reach out and trace her fingers over each one of the ridges on his abdomen.

"Wh-what happened to your shirt?" she asked instead.

"Oh, that." He frowned. "Do you know how disgusting baby food spinach looks? And dear God, it smells even worse. But when it gets on clothes, it's just plain nasty."

She laughed. "It is pretty gross, isn't it?"

"It's horrible." He made a face. "I thought I was going to lose it a couple of times when Mandy decided to take a handful and rub it in her hair."

Heather couldn't stop laughing. "Don't tell me. You set the dish too close to the high chair."

Nodding, he chuckled. "By the time lunch was over, she had more food on her than in her. And I'm positive our daughter could hold her own in a frat house food fight."

"No doubt about it," she agreed, smiling. "Any other problems? How did the diaper changes go?"

"When I finally got her to hold still it went all right. Up until then, it was a little hazardous." He rubbed his flat stomach. "She's got a hell of a kick." His expression turned serious and he fell silent a moment before reaching up to touch her cheek. "Thank you, Heather."

The back of his knuckles stroking her skin sent a shaft of longing all the way to her toes. "Wh-what for?"

"For today." His voice took on a husky quality that stole her breath. "For giving me the chance to get to know my daughter."

Without a second thought, she closed her eyes and leaned into his tender touch. She might have been able to resist had it not been for the sincerity in his tone and the genuine gratefulness in his amazing blue eyes. But no matter how much she tried to fight it, he was the man who had stolen her heart all those months ago and given her a precious baby daughter.

"I want to kiss you, Heather."

His whisper made her feel warm all over. "Th-that probably wouldn't be a good idea."

"Oh, I disagree, I think it's an excellent idea." His firm lips lightly grazing the shell of her ear and his warm breath feathering over her skin caused excited little shivers to course throughout her entire body.

She was flirting with danger. This was Jake Garnier, player extraordinaire. But even as she tried to reason with herself, she swayed toward him.

Apparently, that was all the encouragement he needed because the next thing she knew he wrapped his arms around her and pulled her close. She opened her eyes just in time to watch him slowly, deliberately, lower his head and when his mouth covered hers in tender exploration, she thought she just might melt into a puddle at his feet.

As his tongue stroked her lips apart, her eyes drifted shut again and the intensity of his kiss caused her head to spin. But when he coaxed, demanded and persuaded her to respond, every cell in her body tingled to life and Heather found herself holding on to him for support.

She should stop him. It wasn't smart to kiss the man who obviously hadn't wanted anything more to do with her until he learned that she'd given birth to his daughter. But the thought evaporated when Jake crushed her to him and she felt his hard muscles against her tightening nipples and his insistent arousal pressed into her lower belly.

Her knees threatened to buckle and a swirling hunger began to flow through her when he moved his hand to cup her breast, then chafed the hardened tip through the layers of her clothing. She wanted him with a fierceness that frightened her more than she'd ever thought possible.

Jake must have sensed the change in her because he slowly eased away from the kiss, but continued to hold her close. "We've got plenty of time."

She could deny that having him kiss her, that being in his arms and having his body entangled with hers wasn't what she wanted, too. But they'd both know it was a total lie.

"No, it can't happen, Jake." It was hard to be convincing when his large hand still covered her breast. But she couldn't seem to find the strength to pull free of his arms.

"I'm not going to stand here and argue. Right now, I have to take a shower."

As she watched him retreat to the master suite, Heather couldn't help but wonder if she shouldn't take her daughter and run as fast as she could back to the safety of the carriage house. It was obvious that no matter what she said, he wasn't going to listen to her. And living in such close proximity was going to make resisting him extremely difficult.

But thankfully with the Southern Oaks Cup Classic only two weeks away and all of the activities that preceded it, they were both going to become very busy in a very short time. If she could just hold out a few more days, everything should be fine.

She was going to have to attend to Dancer seven days a week and make sure that he was ready to run the race of his life. And as the owner of the favorite to win the Cup, Jake would be away at the almost non-stop receptions and balls that were held to celebrate the annual event.

With her going to bed early in order to oversee the thoroughbred's dawn exercises and Jake sleeping in after being out late with Louisville's social elite, their paths probably wouldn't cross more than a handful of times. And the few times they did, it would most likely be in a public setting for pictures and publicity for the race.

Then, by the time the festivities came to a close, Jake would no doubt be bored with the comparatively slower pace of Hickory Hills and more than ready to head back to his exciting life in Los Angeles. She and Mandy would move back into the carriage house and once again settle into their comfortable, familiar routine.

As Jake sat in the study thumbing through a pile of invitations to teas, receptions and balls being held in honor of the big race, he frowned. How the hell was he supposed to work things out and reconnect with Heather when he was going to have to attend a string of social events?

But staring at the elaborate print on one of the invitations, a slow smile curved the corners of his mouth. The words "and guest" had him rising from his chair.

"Clara, could you watch Mandy for a few minutes while I walk down to the stables to talk to Heather?" he asked when he entered the kitchen.

"No problem." She smiled when she handed her the baby monitor. "How long has our little angel been down for her nap?"

"About a half hour." He checked his watch. "I'm not sure how long she sleeps, but I'll only be a few minutes."

"Take your time." Clara grinned as she motioned toward Daily seated at the kitchen table peeling a pile of potatoes. "We won't be going anywhere for at least the next two weeks."

"I keep telling you, Grandma. When somebody's grounded, it doesn't mean they have to do stuff like this," the boy complained. "It means they just can't go anywhere."

Jake hid a smile as he left the mansion and walking past the pool, started down the path toward the stables. Since his grandmother learned about his plan for a late night rendezvous, Daily had mucked out stalls, mopped floors, polished silver and performed any other menial task she could think to assign him.

In a few days, the kid would get a bit of a reprieve from doing household chores. Jake had already talked to Clara about having Daily help him with a few projects to improve the place. The housekeeper had readily agreed and expressed her gratitude for

Jake's influence with the boy. It seemed that Daily was having a hard time adjusting to his mother remarrying after the death of his father and she'd sent him to Hickory Hills in an effort to keep him out of trouble.

Shaking his head, Jake couldn't help but wonder what his friends in L.A. would think of that one. With his reputation for partying and entertaining a different woman every night, he was the last person most people would want influencing their teenage boy. But since his arrival at Hickory Hills, Jake had found that he was enjoying the slower, laid-back pace and had started thinking less and less about getting back to the hectic schedule he'd kept for the past several years.

Maybe it had something to do with finding out he'd fathered a child. Or it could be that it was just so vastly different from his usual lifestyle the novelty hadn't worn off yet.

He frowned. So why didn't going back to L.A. sound all that appealing?

As he entered the stable, another thought occurred to him, but he dismissed it. He refused to believe that he might finally be ready to settle down. That was just ludicrous. Of course, he wanted to return to his condo and highly successful law practice. He'd be a fool not to want that.

Greeting Tony and another groom as they attended to one of the thoroughbreds, Jake relegated his self-analysis to the back of his mind. It was amusing to think that he owned over two dozen of the finest animals in the country and he'd never been on the back of horse in his entire life.

"What's up?" Heather asked when he walked into her office. "Is everything all right?"

Jake nodded. "Mandy is taking a nap and Clara is making Daily rue the day he even thought about sneaking out to see his girlfriend by making him peel potatoes for dinner."

Heather's smile sent a shockwave of heat straight to the pit of his belly. "Poor Daily. I doubt that he'll be eager to try that again."

Jake barely managed to suppress his frustrated groan. He seriously doubted she realized just how pretty she looked with soft curls escaping her pony-tail and her creamy cheeks flushed from the early summer heat.

But it was her coral lips that fascinated the hell out of him. Since kissing her outside of Mandy's room two days ago, all he'd been able to think about was doing it again and a whole lot more. And it was the "whole lot more" that was about to drive him over the edge.

"Jake did you hear what I asked?"

"Uh…sorry." Lost in his own misery, he hadn't realized that she'd been talking to him. "What was that again?"

"I asked if you needed something," she said patiently.

Oh, yeah, he needed something all right. But she didn't want to hear what that was.

"As a matter of fact, there is something I need your help with." That was an understatement, he thought sardonically. Forcing himself to focus, he sat down in the chair in front of her desk. "I have a million receptions and a couple of balls over the next two weeks."

She nodded. "That's part of the Southern Oaks Cup celebration and as Dancer's owner, you're expected to make an appearance."

"From the number of invitations I've received, I'm beginning to realize just what a big deal this is," he said, choosing his words carefully. Over the course of the past several years, he'd gotten into the habit of attending parties without a date. Now, he couldn't believe how out of practice he had become at asking a woman out. "And I'd really like for you to go with me."

He watched her open and close her mouth several times before she found her voice. "You can't be serious."

He smiled. "I'm very serious. I wouldn't have asked you to be my date if I weren't."

"I...um, appreciate it, but I can't," she said, her eyes still wide with disbelief.

That wasn't the answer he wanted to hear. "Why not?"

"I'm going to be far too busy overseeing Dancer and preparing for the race to be able to attend." Her smile looked suspiciously relieved when she added, "I'm sorry, but you'll have to go without me."

It was perfectly clear to him why she was turning him down. The more time they spent together, the bigger the possibility she could no longer deny the pull between them. And that was the very reason he was going to insist that she go with him.

"But you would attend the various functions with me if not for your job, right?"

"Well…I…uh…since I'm not about to quit, it's not an issue," she hedged.

He knew he had her and if the look on her pretty face was any indication, she knew it, too.

Rising from the chair, he walked over and called for Tony to come to the office. When the man walked to the door, Jake smiled. "From now until the race is over, you're in charge of the stables. I want Heather free to concentrate on overseeing Dancer's training, preparations for the race and attending social functions."

The man looked as if he thought Jake might be joking. "Me?"

"Yes," Jake answered decisively. "Do you think you can handle the job?"

He watched the man's gaze cut to Heather, then back to him. "Sure. I can handle it, but—"

"Then it's settled." Jake shook Tony's hand. "If anything comes up, you're still to consult with Heather."

When he turned to walk back and lower himself into the chair in front of Heather's desk, she looked as if she might blow a gasket. "What do you think you're doing?"

"I'm relieving you of your other duties until after the race is over." He smiled. "This way you'll be able to focus on Dancer and the race and attend the social side of this thing with me."

"You can't do that to me," she said, standing up to pace back and forth behind the desk.

"Sure I can."

She stopped to glare at him. "I have a signed contract that says otherwise. You may own this place, but I run it. I'm in charge and I call the shots."

"You're still in charge, Heather." He hadn't anticipated that she'd get this upset.

"At least running this farm will look good on my résumé," she muttered.

He narrowed his eyes. "You haven't been looking for a position elsewhere, have you?"

"Not yet," she admitted belligerently. "But you just made the decision to start the search a lot easier."

Rising to his feet, he walked around the desk and took her into his arms. "Look, you're still in charge.

You're still overseeing Dancer's racing career. That hasn't changed. I'm just making it easier for you to concentrate your efforts on him."

"Get real, Jake. We both know the reason you relieved me of the majority of my responsibilities was purely self-serving. You want me to attend the social events with you. That's the only reason you did this."

He took a deep breath. "That's the way it started out. But the more I think about it, the more it makes sense for Dancer to be your top priority now."

"I can't argue that," she grudgingly agreed.

"And won't it make the next two weeks easier if you can turn your sole attention to that goal?"

She slowly nodded.

"I'm sorry I usurped your authority, but I'm used to being the one in charge." He kissed the top of her head. "From now on, I'll consult with you before I make a decision about the stables."

She leaned back to look him square in the eyes and he could tell she was only slightly less furious with him. "You'd better, because if you interfere again, I'm out of here."

If he'd doubted how seriously she took her job before, he didn't now. "Understood. Now, will you please consider attending events with me. It would be nice to have someone I know at my side."

"There isn't a shy bone in your body. You'll do just fine without me."

He smiled as he brushed an errant strand of golden brown hair from her soft cheek. "Yes, but I want you with me."

"I told you, I'm not one of your diversions while you're here," she stated flatly.

She wasn't going to give in easily. But then he wasn't, either. "Would you at least think about going with me?" he whispered close to her ear.

Staring at him for what seemed an eternity, she finally nodded. "I'll consider it, but I'm not promising anything."

Satisfied that his plan to spend more time with her had a chance, Jake lowered his mouth to hers to seal the deal with a kiss. His blood pressure skyrocketed as he slowly caressed her lips with his, and he decided he could easily become addicted to her sweetness as he savored the taste of her.

When he traced the seam of her mouth to deepen the kiss, he took advantage of her soft sigh and slipped inside to stroke her tongue with his. Teasing and coaxing, he encouraged her to explore him, as well, and when she tentatively acquainted herself with him, Jake felt as if a fire had been ignited in the pit of his belly.

But it was the feel of her breasts pressed to his chest, her nipples scoring his skin through the layers of their clothing, that caused his body to harden so fast it left him feeling lightheaded. He moved his hands down her back to the flare of her hips. Pulling her forward allowed her to feel the effect she had on him, how she made him want her. She whimpered softly and sagged against him, letting him know without words that she desired him as much as he did her.

Unfortunately, his timing was lousy. They were in her office in the stable with several people close by. And going back to the mansion was out of the question.

Reluctantly easing away from the kiss, Jake took a deep breath as he leaned back to stare down at her. He didn't think he'd ever seen a more beautiful sight. Heather's porcelain cheeks were flushed and her eyes were glazed with the haze of unfulfilled desire.

"I suppose I should let you get back to work now," he finally managed to get out through his dry throat. Before she could gather her thoughts and tear into him over kissing her again, he released her and, walking to the door, added, "Our first reception is this evening. You can fill me in on our host and hostess on the drive over to their place."

# Five

Heather accepted the hand Jake offered as she got out of his Ferrari in front of the home of John and Martha Wainwright, then waited for him to hand his keys to the valet. She was still upset with him over his disregard for her authority at the farm, but the more she thought about it, the more she realized attending these social events with him could work to her advantage. If she did have to look for a position elsewhere, the contacts she made at receptions like this one could prove invaluable.

"So tell me about these people," he said as he cupped her elbow and they walked the short distance to the tall, carved-oak front doors of the estate.

"John Wainwright is president of the Southern

Oaks Bank and Trust and Martha is the treasurer of the local ladies' club," she said, quickly filling him in on their host and hostess. "Neither of them have the slightest interest in horses or the Classic. But they would both have a coronary before they passed up an opportunity to host a reception for it."

"In other words, they're all about showing off with a big party and getting a mention in the society column."

"Exactly."

When he handed the doorman their invitation, the man smiled broadly and swung one of the entry doors wide. "Welcome to Waincrest, Mr. Garnier." He nodded and gave her a wink. "And Miss Heather."

"Hi, Hank. How is Mae?" she asked, smiling.

The man's grin widened. "She's doing just fine, Miss Heather. Thank you for asking."

As they followed his directions past a sweeping staircase and out a set of French doors onto the terrace, she felt as if she'd stepped into a fairy tale. The place was decorated with a canopy of tiny white lights, white wrought-iron patio furniture and huge bouquets of red and white roses in marble urns. Clearly, the Wainwrights had spared no expense in transforming their lawn into a very elegant cocktail party.

"That's our host and hostess," she said, discreetly nodding toward a couple standing by the bar.

"This is why I needed you with me," Jake said,

leaning close. "You know who all these people are and what role they play in all of this hoopla."

She rolled her eyes. "Like you wouldn't have figured it out on your own."

When a waiter carrying a silver tray with glasses of champagne stopped in front of them, Jake removed two of the flutes, then handed one to her. "If I remember correctly, I think this is how we met."

She swallowed hard when his fingers lingered on hers a little longer than necessary and a feeling of déjà vu swept through her. He'd walked over to her, handed her a glass of champagne and the rest was history.

He leaned close. "Do you think the evening will end the same way it did that night?"

"With me pregnant?"

Jake's teasing smile faded. "I didn't mean *that*. But I'll be damned if I'm sorry it happened. We wouldn't have Mandy if it hadn't."

She could tell he was completely sincere, and she had to agree. "She's brought more joy into my life than I could have ever imagined."

Before either of them had a chance to say anything further, John Wainwright walked over to greet them. "You must be the owner of Stormy Dancer," the man said, turning up the wattage on his smile. Almost as an afterthought, he nodded at her. "Miss McGwire."

Wainwright wasn't interested in talking to her and

she knew why. His bank handled the accounts for Hickory Hills and he wasn't going to waste his time with a lowly farm manager when he could schmooze with the owner of one of the premier stables in the entire country.

As the man engaged Jake in a conversation about becoming a member of the local country club, Heather quietly excused herself and started to walk away.

Jake put his hand on her arm to stop her. "Where do you think you're going?"

Smiling, she pointed toward the buffet table. "I'll be over there."

She could tell he wasn't happy with the way John Wainwright had dismissed her as insignificant. But she really didn't mind being excluded from their conversation. She was far more comfortable talking to the Wainwrights' staff than she was mingling with people who thought they were better than everyone else.

"Dear, would you mind helping me?" a small, elderly woman asked politely. With a cane in one hand and a mint julep in the other, the poor woman had no way of carrying her plate of appetizers.

Smiling, Heather shook her head. "I don't mind at all. Where are you sitting?"

"As far away from these pompous asses as possible," she replied, her expression so sweet that Heather thought she might have misheard.

"Excuse me?"

"You heard right, dear. I called them pompous asses," the older woman repeated proudly. "I've finally reached the age where I speak my mind and don't give a fig what people think. Now, come. Let's find a place to sit and get acquainted."

When Heather followed the elderly lady to an empty table away from the majority of the crowd, she helped the woman get settled. "Is there anything else you need, Mrs...."

"Wainwright." The old lady shook her head disgustedly. "My son is the windbag who snubbed you in favor of kissing up to your young man." She patted the chair beside her. "Sit, dear. I need someone to talk to who doesn't act like they're something they're not." She gave a disgusted snort. "I just hate when John and Martha throw one of these receptions. They put on such airs, it's a downright disgrace."

Heather didn't know what to say. But she couldn't help but like the elderly woman and her candid observations.

"It's all right, dear." The old woman patted Heather's hand. "I have no illusions about how important most of these people *think* they are. And my son and daughter-in-law are the two biggest ducks in the puddle."

"Well, your son is the president of Southern Oaks Bank and Trust."

"Pish posh. It doesn't matter what job somebody ends up with, they should never forget where they came from." Mrs. Wainwright grinned. "I'll bet you didn't know that John grew up the son of a tobacco farmer who was land rich and dirt poor." She pointed an arthritic finger toward Jake. "But your young man seems to be different. You can tell he's got money, but he doesn't appear to act like he's better than everyone else. I'll bet he hasn't forgotten who he really is and where he came from."

Heather stared at Jake. She still knew very little about him. Busy getting ready for the race, she hadn't had the opportunity to ask where he grew up, about his childhood or his family.

Were his mother and father still alive? Did he have siblings? Could Mandy have family that Heather knew nothing about?

She didn't have a clue. But she had every intention of finding out.

As Heather continued to think about it, she had to admit that Mrs. Wainwright was correct in her assessment of him. Jake had never made her or anyone at the farm feel as if they were beneath him. Even Clara had commented that he went out of his way to make everyone feel comfortable.

Heather had watched him with the grooms and stable boys and he never failed to greet them by name or stop and talk to them for a few minutes. And he was probably the only billionaire she'd ever heard of who sat at the kitchen table to eat his meals with his housekeeper, her teenage grandson and his farm manager.

"Are you ready to thank our host and hostess for a nice evening and head home?"

Heather jumped. Lost in thought, she hadn't realized that Jake had ended his conversation with the bank president and crossed the lawn to join her and the man's mother.

Introducing him to the elderly Mrs. Wainwright, she smiled. "It was nice chatting with you."

"It was my pleasure, dear." Mrs. Wainwright placed a bony hand on Heather's arm and motioned for her to lean close. "You hang on to your young man," she said in confidence. "Mark my words, he's the real deal."

"Thank you, Mrs. Wainwright." She smiled. "I'll try to remember that."

After bidding the Wainwrights a good evening, Jake waited until he and Heather were seated in his car before he apologized. "I'm sorry, honey."

"What for?" She looked thoroughly bewildered and so damned beautiful it was all he could do to keep from stopping the car and taking her into his arms.

"Wainwright had no right to ignore you the way he did." When the man dismissed Heather as if she didn't exist, a protectiveness he'd never known he possessed had consumed him and Jake had wanted to punch the bastard in his big pretentious nose.

They fell silent for some time before he felt Heather staring at him. "What?"

"Tell me more about yourself."

Glancing her way, he frowned. "What do you want to know?"

"Everything. Where did you grow up? Do you have siblings?" She laid her soft hand on his thigh and he had to concentrate to keep from steering the car into the ditch. "Does Mandy have an extended family?"

"What brought this on?" he asked, covering her hand with his to keep her from moving it. He liked when she touched him.

"Jake, we have a child together and beyond the fact that you're a successful divorce attorney in Los Angeles, I know very little else about you," she said quietly.

"There's no big mystery. My siblings and I were born and raised in San Francisco. I have an identical twin brother named Luke—"

"My God, there are two of you?" She sounded truly shocked.

Grinning he nodded. "But don't worry. He's always been the quiet, more serious one of us."

"In other words, your exact opposite." She looked thoughtful. "Is he married?"

"As a matter of fact, he just got married a few

months ago. He and his wife, Haley, are expecting their first child in about six and a half months." To his surprise, Jake found that he liked sharing details about his family with Heather. "And we have a sister, Arielle. She's ten years younger. She got married last month and is five months pregnant with twin boys."

Heather was silent so long, he thought she might have fallen asleep. "I'm so happy that Mandy is going to have aunts, uncles and cousins." She paused. "What about grandparents? Are your parents still alive?"

"No, our mother was killed in a car accident when Luke and I were twenty." He took a deep breath. No matter how long it had been, he still missed the woman who had give him and his siblings life.

"I'm so sorry. What about your father?"

He snorted. "We only met our father once. After he made our mother pregnant with me and Luke, he took off and she didn't see him again until we were almost ten. That's when he showed up, stuck around only long enough to make Mom pregnant with Arielle, then took off again." It was his turn to pause. "We recently got word that he was killed in a boating accident a couple of years ago."

"Who finished raising your sister after your mother died?" she asked, sounding genuinely concerned.

"Luke and I were in college and managed to work out a pretty good system. He would work one semester and take over most of Arielle's care while I went to school. Then I'd lay out the next semester, get a job and I'd be responsible for her while he attended classes."

"My God, Jake, that had to have been so hard for both of you." She turned her hand, palm up, to clasp his. "Did you try to get in touch with your father to see if he would send money to help out with your sister?"

Stopping the car at the entrance to Hickory Hills, he used the remote Clara had given him to open the wide iron gates. "We tried, but it proved to be impossible. We didn't even know his real name."

Her mouth dropped open. "He lied about who he was?"

Jake nodded. "We didn't find that out and who he really was until we were told he was dead."

When he drove the car through the gates, he pushed the button to swing them shut and as they traveled the long oak-lined drive, he decided to omit his newly discovered grandmother's name. Emerald Larson was Mandy's great-grandmother but he still wasn't comfortable with the fact or with the way she manipulated her grandchildren.

"Mandy does have a great-grandmother," he said, watching Heather from the corner of his eye. "We learned about her at the same time we found out about our father's death."

She smiled. "It's nice that you finally found each other."

"More like she found us." He shrugged. "She knew how wild and unsettled her son was and after he died, she had a team of investigators search to see if he had any children so that she could set things right with all of us."

"That's when she got in touch with you and your siblings?" Heather asked, seemingly fascinated with what he was telling her.

"Among others."

He could tell from her expression that Heather was thoroughly shocked. "You mean...he fathered more children than just you and your siblings?"

"It turns out our father took the biblical passage where it says 'Be fruitful and multiply' to heart." He smiled as he parked the car in the circular drive in front of the mansion. "He also fathered three other sons by three different women in the ten years between fathering me and Luke and Arielle."

Her eyes grew even wider. "Wow! He certainly was...um, active."

"To say the least."

Jake got out of the car and as he walked around to open the passenger door for her, he couldn't help but see the parallel between the way he'd been living his life and the way his father had. And he wasn't overly proud of it. But he was different from his father in one very important way. Jake was going to be there for Mandy where his father had failed his children in every way possible.

When Heather got out of the car to stand in front of him, he didn't hesitate to put his arms around her. "I know it seems like I've been living my life a lot like my father did, and maybe to a certain extent, I have. But let me assure you, I'll always be there for Mandy…and for you."

"Jake—"

"I mean it, Heather. I'm not the irresponsible jerk my father was."

Deciding that enough had been said about his notorious father and atypical family, he let his gaze travel from her silky hair swept up into a stylish twist, down the length of her black strapless cocktail dress, to her impossibly high, black heels. In L.A. they had a colorful phrase for those kind of shoes and he seriously doubted that she realized some women wore them to send a message that they were open to a night of unbridled passion.

Groaning, he raised his head to rest his forehead against hers. "Do you have any idea how sexy you are? How beautiful?"

Before she had the chance to speak, Jake teased and coaxed her mouth with his own until she granted him the access he sought. But he was completely unprepared and not at all disappointed when Heather took control of the kiss and touched her tongue to his.

At first tentative, her shy stroking sent electric sparks to every nerve in his being. As she gained confidence and engaged him in a game of advance and retreat, the sparks touched off a flame in the pit of his belly that quickly had him wondering if he was about to burn to a cinder.

The reaction of his body was instantaneous. He hadn't become aroused this fast since his teens.

With his knees threatening to buckle and his head swimming from a serious lack of blood to the brain, he reluctantly broke the caress. If he didn't put an end to the kiss, and right now, he was in real danger of making love to her right there on the steps of the veranda.

"Honey…I can't believe…I'm going to say this." He stopped long enough to draw some much needed air into his lungs. "Unless you're ready to go upstairs with me—to my room, my bed—we'd better call it a night."

He watched her passion-flushed cheeks turn a deep shade of rose a moment before she shook her head. "I'm sorry…I… Not yet." She suddenly clamped her mouth shut, then took a step away from him, then another. "I mean…no. That's not going to happen."

When Heather turned and fled up the steps, across the veranda and disappeared into the house, Jake reached up to unknot his tie and unbutton the collar of his shirt. Then, stuffing his hands in his pants pockets, took off at a brisk walk back down the long drive toward the entrance gates.

He couldn't believe how the evening had turned

out. He wasn't in the habit of divulging personal information to the women he dated. It kept things from becoming complicated when he went his way and they went theirs.

But Heather was different. For reasons he didn't care to contemplate, he wanted her to know all about him. And he wanted to learn everything about her. What had inspired her to choose her career? Did she have siblings? Were her parents still alive?

Shaking his head, he fell into a steady pace as he started back toward the house. He had no idea what had gotten into him. Yet as he got better acquainted with his only child, he had every intention of getting close to her mother, as well.

Checking on her daughter sleeping peacefully in her crib, Heather crossed the hall and, entering the bedroom she'd been using since Jake moved her and Mandy into the mansion, closed the door. What on earth had possessed her to take control of that kiss? And why had she the same as told him that at some point she would be ready to make love with him again? Had she lost her mind?

As she removed her heels and unzipped her dress, she thought about the details he'd shared with her about his family. There was a lot more to Jake Garnier than first met the eye or that he allowed people to see.

He was a self-made man who hadn't always had

an easy life. He'd been there right along with his twin brother to step in and accept the responsibility of raising their younger sister, while still managing to complete his education. That had been a monumental undertaking and she could tell that he wouldn't have considered doing it any other way. He and his siblings had struggled to stay together and they'd made it. That certainly wasn't something a self-indulgent playboy would do.

She slipped out of her dress and, hanging it in the closet, took down her hair and changed into her nightgown. When she climbed into bed, she closed her eyes and hugged one of the pillows tightly against her.

The more she learned about Jake, the more she admired him. Considering she was finding it almost impossible to resist him, that was extremely dangerous. She couldn't afford to let go of her preconceived notion that he cared little or nothing about anyone but himself. If she did, there was a very real possibility that she and her daughter would both end up getting hurt.

Lying there hugging the pillow, she must have drifted off to sleep because the next thing she knew, her daughter's cries coming through the baby monitor awakened her. She tossed the pillow aside and, getting out of bed, reached for her robe. But the sound of Jake's voice stopped her.

"What's wrong, Mandy? Did my little honey

bunny have a bad dream?" He must have taken the spare receiver to his room before he turned in for the night.

As she listened to him comfort their daughter, tears filled her eyes and spilled down her cheeks. It was clear from the tone of his voice that he loved Mandy, and Heather knew as surely as she knew her own name that he would be just as committed and protective of their daughter as any father could possibly be.

Without a second thought, she quietly opened her door and, tiptoeing across the hall, watched Jake gently cradle Mandy to his bare chest. She waited until he put their sleeping daughter back in the crib, then walked out into the hall. "I appreciate your trying to let me sleep."

Running his hand through his thick hair, he shook his head. "Too bad it didn't work out."

When they both fell silent, Heather found it hard not to stare. Dressed in nothing but a pair of navy silk pajama bottoms, he looked absolutely…yummy. She suddenly felt warm all over.

"Heather, are you all right?"

"I…um, yes." She needed to make her escape while she still had the presence of mind to do it.

His slow smile said that he knew exactly what she'd been thinking. "I like the way you look, too." Reaching out, he traced one of the thin spaghetti straps of her gown with his index finger. "You make turquoise look real good, honey."

"I thought that was supposed to be...the other way around," she said, realizing that she'd forgotten all about her robe when she'd heard Jake talking to the baby. "Isn't the color supposed to compliment the person wearing it?"

"Not in your case, Heather." He trailed his finger down the strap to the gown's rounded neckline. "You make everything you wear sexy."

A shiver flowed through her when the tip of his finger lightly grazed the slope of her breast. "I'm... going back to...my room."

He took her into his arms. "I'd rather you stay with me."

"Out here in the hall?"

Staring up at him, she knew she was playing with fire. The feel of him holding her and the rich sound of his voice lowered to an intimate timbre caused an ache that she knew for certain only he could ease.

"I was thinking more like my room." His seductive smile sent her pulse into overdrive.

What she wanted was to go with him. What she needed was peace of mind. And that would be in serious jeopardy if she let her heart overrule her head.

She took a deep breath as she summoned every ounce of strength she possessed. "I want you to go to your room and...I'll go to mine."

"Are you certain that's what you really want, Heather?"

They both knew she was telling a huge lie. The last thing she wanted was to go back alone to the big empty bed across the hall. But making love with Jake would only add another wrinkle to their already complicated situation, not to mention pose a serious risk to her heart.

"Y-yes." Turning to go across the hall to her room, she wished she'd sounded more convincing. "Good night, Jake."

When he placed his hand on her shoulder to stop her, the look in his amazing blue gaze caused her heart to beat double time. "You can only run from this—from us—for so long." He leaned forward to kiss her with such tenderness she thought she might do something stupid like give in. "Sleep well, sweet Heather."

As she watched him stroll down the hall toward the master suite, she had to lean against the door frame to keep her knees from folding beneath her. How on earth was she ever going to be able to resist such blatant sexuality?

She somehow managed to walk into the bedroom and close the door. If it was just a matter of physical attraction, she was pretty sure she'd be successful. But the more she learned about Jake and the more she saw how much he cared for their daughter, the closer she came to listening to her heart. And that was something she couldn't let happen again.

She climbed into bed and hugged the pillow close again. There was no doubt about it. If she intended to survive Jake's visit to Hickory Hills, she was going to have to keep her emotions in check. She was in danger of losing a lot more than her heart if she didn't. They still had yet to discuss how they were going to raise Mandy, and considering the high-handed way he'd relieved her of most of her duties, she might end up losing her job.

But as she lay there thinking about how it felt when he touched her, held her, she knew that keeping her wits about her was going to be all but impossible to do. She was falling for him all over again and there didn't seem to be anything she could do to stop it.

# Six

"Where's Heather?" Jake asked when he walked into the kitchen and found Clara feeding the baby breakfast.

"Tony called. There was a problem down at the stables with one of the horses and he wanted her to come down to assess the situation." The housekeeper shook her head. "He knows Heather would never forgive him if he hadn't let her know about it."

Jake frowned. He'd put Tony in charge to free Heather from having to deal with this sort of thing until after the race. "Is there something wrong with Dancer?"

"No. I think she said one of the other studs has a really nasty cut on its pastern." She spooned a mouthful of cereal into Mandy's open mouth. "Heather's almost as good as a vet when it comes to taking care of horses and I'm pretty sure Tony wanted her to take a look at the injury to see how bad it is."

Clara might as well have been speaking a foreign language for all he understood about where the horse was injured. "How did she learn so much about horses?" he asked as he grabbed a mug from the cabinet, then poured himself a cup of coffee.

"Bless her heart, she learned from the best," the housekeeper said, smiling fondly. "Before he died five years ago, her dad, George, was the manager here. From the time she was old enough to walk, she followed him around like a shadow and soaked up everything he knew about horses."

Fascinated by the details he was learning about Heather, Jake leaned against the kitchen counter. "What about her mother? Is she still around?"

Clara snorted. "No, and I say good riddance. She was a wild one, always looking for a good time. She took off when Heather was six and they never heard from her again."

It sounded to him like Heather's mother and his father were a lot alike—narcissistic and completely irresponsible. "I think I'll walk down to the stable and see what's going on. Would you mind watching Mandy until Heather and I get back?"

"Not at all." Clara grinned as she wiped the baby's face. "Take all the time you need. The only thing I have to do this morning is come up with another list of chores to keep Daily busy after he finishes mucking out the stalls."

Chuckling, Jake wondered how much longer the woman was going to make the boy suffer for his lapse of judgment. "I have another project that I'd like his help with. Do you think you could pencil that in on the schedule for tomorrow?"

Clara nodded. "Will you need him all day?"

"Probably several days. Will that be a problem?"

"Not at all." She smiled. "What have you got up your sleeve this time?"

"When we moved Heather and the baby, I noticed the carriage house could use a fresh coat of paint and some new carpet."

As Jake left the house and walked the distance to the stables, his thoughts returned to Heather and he couldn't help but wonder how she'd slept the night before. If he was taking bets, he'd wager that she hadn't gotten any more sleep than he had.

Entering the stable, he followed the sound of a loud commotion. What had been so important that Tony felt the need to call Heather?

"Hold him while I get him tranquilized."

Jake automatically turned at the sound of Heather's voice inside one of the stalls and it felt as if his heart came up into his throat. As he watched, she, Tony and another groom jumped back just in time to keep from being kicked by a very large, extremely agitated horse.

"Heather, get out of there." He tossed the coffee cup onto a pile of straw and reached to open the stall's half door.

"Don't you dare open that door," she warned. "Just stay back. We've got this under control."

It didn't appear that they had everything in hand. It looked as if someone was about to get seriously hurt. The thought that it might be Heather had his heart hammering so hard that he thought he'd surely end up with a few cracked ribs.

When Tony and the other man finally caught hold of the thoroughbred's halter, Heather moved swiftly to jab a long needle into the animal's shoulder. The horse lurched to one side, then kicked the back of the stall with a blow that Jake knew for certain would have killed someone had it connected with one of the humans inside the enclosure. But just when he thought all hell was going to break loose, Heather and the grooms managed to open the half door and escape.

Fear ignited an anger in him that quickly flared out of control and he was itching for a confrontation. "What the hell do you think you were doing in there?" he demanded when she stood safely in front of him.

"The job you pay me to do."

He stubbornly shook his head. "I pay a veterinarian to attend injured horses. And if the size of his bills are any indication, I pay him quite well."

As he and Heather glared at each other, Jake noticed Tony and the other man hurrying toward the far end of the barn. They apparently decided that retreat was the better part of valor.

"For your information, the vet *is* on the way." Her aqua eyes sparkled with anger and he didn't think he'd ever seen her look prettier.

"Then why were you in the stall? Why didn't you wait for Dr. Pennington to get here?"

"Because Magic needed a sedative immediately," she shot back. "We couldn't run the risk of him making the injury worse."

"I don't care," he said angrily. "You could have gotten yourself killed."

"I've been around horses all my life and I know what I'm doing," she insisted. "Besides, that horse is a full brother to Dancer and almost as valuable as he is. His stud fees alone are going to make you a fortune once he's retired from racing."

Reaching out, Jake took her by the shoulders. "Don't you understand? It's not about the money, Heather. Your safety is far more important to me than any money I could make off of a damned horse."

She stared at him for several long seconds before her stormy expression began to ease a bit. "Honestly, I really wasn't in as much danger as it might have seemed, Jake."

He crushed her to him. "Even the slightest chance of you being hurt in any way is one chance too many, honey."

As his heart slowly returned to a more normal beat, he couldn't get over the fear that had coursed through him when he saw the horse come so close to kicking her. It had rivaled the feeling he'd experienced a few days ago when he'd awakened to find his napping daughter missing from where she'd fallen asleep on his chest.

Before he could analyze what that might mean, he lowered his head to cover Heather's mouth with his. He told himself that he needed to reassure himself that she was indeed all right. Yet the truth of the matter was he'd become quite good at looking for reasons to kiss her.

Soft and pliant, her lips immediately fused with his as she wrapped her arms around his neck. But when she used the tip of her tongue to invite him to deepen the kiss, her eager response to the caress sent blood surging through his veins and his body hardened so fast it made him dizzy.

As he slipped inside and teased, he slid his hands from her back to her delightful little blue jeans-clad bottom and tried to pull her even closer. But an insistent nudge against his legs had him breaking the kiss to look down at the big dog trying to work his way between them.

"Thank God Nemo came along when he did."

Heather's cheeks colored a pretty pink as she glanced down the wide aisle to see if anyone had been watching.

"I thought you were supposed to be man's best friend," Jake groused when he bent to pick up his discarded coffee cup. He scratched behind the big dog's ears. "How would you like it if I interrupted you and one of your female friends?"

"Since he's been neutered, I doubt he'd care," she said dryly.

"Nemo, buddy, I'm so sorry to hear that," Jake said sympathetically.

She looked confused. "Why are you sorry he's been neutered?"

"It's a guy thing." Jake shook his head. "You wouldn't understand."

"The vet just arrived," Tony called from the opposite end of the stable, drawing their attention back to the matter at hand.

"Heather and I are going back up to the house," Jake said before she could answer or find an excuse to stick around. "You assist him with whatever he needs."

"No problem, boss."

"I'm not going anywhere," she stated. "My job is to stay right here and see to Stormy Magic's welfare."

"Dr. Pennington has arrived and Tony will see that he takes good care of whatever treatment the animal needs." Turning her, Jake put his arm around her shoulders and started walking them from the stable. "Besides, if you'll remember, we have a dinner meeting with a couple of the other owners and then the Southern Oaks Ball to attend this evening."

"You could go without me."

"Nope. You agreed to be my date for these things. It's too late to back out now."

She shook her head. "It was more like you pulled rank and told me I was going."

He chuckled. "Whatever. You'll need to start getting ready early."

"Why? We're not meeting the other owners until seven this evening."

"I was contacted this morning by the television network carrying the race. They want to interview us before dinner and get some footage for their *Meet the Owners* prerace segment."

"I don't own Dancer. You do. There's no reason for me to be included in that." She shrugged from beneath his arm and stopping, glared at him. "Right after he was named the favorite to win the Classic, they showed up here to tape his daily exercises and grooming. They interviewed me then and I told them everything there is to know about Dancer." She shook her head. "This particular fifteen minutes of fame is all yours."

When Jake helped her out of the back of the limousine, Heather felt as if she'd stepped right into the middle of a three-ring circus. Cameras whirred and reporters called out questions as they walked along the carpeted runway toward the entrance of one of the oldest and most prestigious hotels in Louisville.

"This is just like a Hollywood premiere," Jake said, placing his hand to her back to guide her.

"And the very reason I would have preferred staying at home," she muttered. They'd spent an hour and a half before dinner being interviewed by the television network as well as a couple of reporters from the print media. She was more than ready to escape the spotlight.

"What was that, honey?" he asked, leaning close.

"It's not important." She wasn't surprised he hadn't been able to hear her. The noise was almost deafening.

Thankfully they left most of the chaos behind as they crossed the lobby to enter the Grand Ballroom. She waited while Jake presented the doorman with his invitation, then walking into the ornate room, looked around. The light from the massive crystal chandeliers caused the gold accents on the pristine white walls to take on a rich glow and complemented the heavy floor-to-ceiling red velvet drapes. As she continued to scan the room, she spotted a few of the same guests that had attended the Wainwrights' reception along with several well-known celebrities and foreign dignitaries.

"Is that who I think it is?" Jake asked as a sheikh and his entourage strolled past them.

She nodded. "That's Sheikh Kalid Al-Kahra. He owns Dancer's biggest competition."

"Do you think we have anything to worry about?" Jake asked.

"Not a chance." She couldn't stop her smug smile. "The sheikh's jockey has a tendency to take the horses he's riding to the lead right out of the gate and doesn't let up. By the time they reach the home stretch, the horse has nothing left for the sprint to the finish."

"I'm glad that jockey is riding the sheikh's horse and not ours," Jake said, grinning.

"The previous owner of Hickory Hills demanded the best. That's why we have Miguel Santana wearing our silks." She nodded toward a group standing off to the side of the orchestra. "See that distinguished-looking gentleman over there with all the medals and ribbons? He's the Crown Prince of Marunda. He owns the long shot."

"The Wainwright affair was small potatoes compared to the company we're keeping this evening," Jake said, accepting champagne for both of them from a passing waiter. "There are some very impressive pedigrees here this evening."

"I suppose you could say that." She accepted the sparkling wine he handed her and took a sip. "But I'm more impressed by the horses than I am with the people owning them."

He looked thoughtful. "You really mean that, don't you?"

She nodded. "Owners like the sheikh and the prince were born into their positions in life. They didn't have to work to get where they are. But every horse starts out the same. They may have impressive bloodlines, but they still have to work and prove themselves on the track. That's something to be admired."

They fell silent for several moments before she felt him watching her.

"Is something wrong?"

"Not at all." His smile caused her pulse to speed up. "Do you realize you're the most beautiful woman here tonight?"

"I really hadn't given it much thought," she said truthfully.

She had, however, thought a lot about how handsome *he* was. Dressed in a tuxedo she knew for certain hadn't come off of a rack, he looked absolutely amazing.

When a beautiful young woman stepped up to the microphone in front of the orchestra and began to sing the song "At Last," Jake set both of their glasses on a nearby table. "Let's dance."

He took her hand and leading her out onto the dance floor, took her into his arms. The awareness suddenly arcing between them was spellbinding. Gazing into the other's eyes, neither spoke as the orchestra played and the young woman sang about finally finding love. Jake held her close, and swaying in time to the music, Heather knew that she'd remember the moment for the rest of her life.

When the song ended, the orchestra immediately played the beginning notes of another slow, dreamy love song and he pulled her more fully to him. Resting her head against his broad chest, she closed her eyes. She'd never felt more cherished, more secure than she did at that very moment in Jake's arms.

"Honey, I want you more right now than I've ever wanted anything in my entire life," he whispered close to her ear.

His warm breath caused a shiver to course through her. She could deny that she didn't want him just as much, but she was tired of lying. From the moment he arrived at the farm, she'd fought what she knew now to be the inevitable. Jake's touch, his drugging kisses and being held in his arms had worn down her defenses, and she'd lost the battle she'd waged with herself. She wanted him just as much now as she had the night they'd conceived Mandy.

Leaning back to stare up at him, the heat in his cobalt gaze stole her breath.

"How long are we expected to stay at this thing?" he asked.

Her heart sped up. "We've put in an appearance. That's all that's expected."

"Then what do you say we call it an evening and

go home?" The promising look he gave her sent excitement coursing through her veins.

Before she could answer, he led her off the dance floor and out of the ballroom straight to the concierge desk. Requesting that their limousine be sent to the front entrance, Jake helped her into the backseat. He raised the window between them and the driver, then gathered her into his arms.

Touching her chin with his index finger, he smiled when their gazes met. "You do know what's going to happen when we get back to the farm?"

Her smile robbed him of breath. "Yes."

Crushing her to him, he covered her mouth with his and it suddenly felt as if the temperature in the car went up a good ten degrees. As she put her arms around his neck, she parted her lips and he didn't hesitate to deepen the kiss.

Her eager response sent blood surging through his veins and he didn't think twice about slipping his hand inside the low cut neckline of her evening gown. Caressing her breast, he touched the beaded tip with his thumb. Her moan fueled the fire building in his belly, but when she moved her hand upward from where it rested on his thigh, the rush of heat tightening his groin made him feel as if the top of his head might just come off. He would have liked nothing more than to strip her of the sexy dress and make love to her right then and there. But he hadn't made out in the backseat of car since he was in his teens and he'd forgotten just how uncomfortable it could be.

Breaking the kiss, Jake breathed in some much needed oxygen as he removed his hand, rearranged her dress, then tucked her to his side. As much as he needed her at that moment, he didn't want their lovemaking to be rushed. He wanted their first time together again to be special.

When she snuggled against him and rested her palm on his chest, he covered her hand with his. The ride to Hickory Hills seemed to take twice as long as it should have and by the time the chauffeur stopped the limo in the circular drive in front of the mansion, Jake felt as if he had enough adrenaline running through his veins to run a marathon. Without waiting for the driver, he opened the door and helped Heather out of the car.

Neither spoke as they walked the short distance to the veranda and climbed the steps. Opening the door, Jake stood back for Heather to enter and once they stood inside the foyer, he put his arms around her.

"Is Clara babysitting Mandy in her quarters for the night?"

She nodded. "She volunteered and since I wasn't sure how long we would be out this evening, I took her up on the offer."

Kissing her until they both gasped for breath, he

slipped his arm around her waist. "Let's go upstairs, honey."

When they climbed the stairs and started down the hall toward the master suite, he forced himself not to pick her up and sprint the short distance. He wanted her with a driving urgency. But he focused his entire attention on taking things slowly and refreshing her memory of how good they'd been together in Los Angeles.

Entering his bedroom, he guided her over to the side of the bed, then turning on the bedside lamp, gathered her into his arms. He kissed her forehead, her eyes and the tip of her nose.

"I'm going to kiss you all over and by the time we're finished there won't be a single inch I haven't loved."

As he nibbled his way from the hollow behind her ear down her delicate throat to her collarbone, he reached behind her to unzip her cream-colored sequined gown. When the garment lay in a glittering pool at her feet, his heart stalled at the sight of her white lacy garter belt, sheer nylons and spike heels. He didn't know a man alive who didn't have some sort of fantasy about a woman wearing one of those little scraps of lace and a pair of impossibly high heels.

"If I'd known you were wearing this, we'd have left after that first dance," he said, meaning it.

Her sultry smile sent his blood pressure off the

charts as she stepped away from the gown. "When I get dressed to go out, I like feeling feminine."

He grinned. "We'll have to start going out more often."

Releasing the garters, Jake bent to slowly slide his hands down one of her thighs, taking the sheer hose past her knee and down her slender calf. He lifted her foot to remove her shoe, then pulled the nylon off and tossed it to the side. He did the same thing with her other leg and as he straightened, he leisurely ran his hands up along her thighs, enjoying the feel of her smooth skin beneath his palms.

As he raised his head to capture her mouth with his, he unfastened the garter belt and added it to the growing pile of clothing. Her soft, moist lips clung to his and he knew he'd never tasted anything quite as enticing.

He broke the kiss and holding her gaze with his, made quick work of unhooking her strapless bra. When it fell to the floor, his breath lodged in his lungs at the sight of her perfect breasts. Taking the weight of them in his palms, he watched her close her eyes and a blissful look come over her as he chafed the tips with his thumbs.

"You're so beautiful, so perfect."

"So are you," she said, bringing her hands up to slip them beneath the shoulders of his tuxedo jacket. Sliding them down his arms, she took his coat with her and it soon joined her clothing on the floor.

His heart hammered hard against his ribs as she toyed with the studs on the front of his shirt, then slowly released them one by one. When she parted the linen to place her hands on his chest, her delicate touch caused him to harden to an almost painful state.

"I've wanted to do this since returning from my meeting at Churchill Downs the other day," she admitted as she explored him.

"Not as much as I've wanted you to, honey."

He closed his eyes and enjoyed her fingers tracing the pads of his pectoral muscles and the ridges of his belly. But when she traced the line of hair from his navel all the way down to the waistband of his slacks, his eyes snapped open as a shaft of heat shot straight through him.

Quickly reaching to stop her, he shook his head. "I love the way your hands feel on my body, but I'd rather not start this party without you."

She raised her gaze to meet his and the need he detected in the aqua depths robbed him of breath. "It's been so long," she said breathlessly.

"I know, honey."

He kissed each one of her fingertips before he placed her hands on his shoulders, then brought his to rest at her waist. Staring down at her, he ran his index finger along the waistband of her panties and watched her eyes darken with desire.

Without a word, he slipped his fingers beneath the

elastic and sliding his hands down, bent to remove the scrap of satin. When she stepped out of them and he straightened to face her, his heart stalled at the look she gave him just before she reached out to unfasten the waistband of his trousers.

Before she caused him to have a coronary, he stepped back and made quick work of removing his shirt and pants. But when he reached to remove his boxers, she stopped him.

"Do you mind?" The sound of her voice slid over him like a fine piece of silk.

"Not at all, honey," he said, grinning. "You're doing just fine."

Their gazes remained locked as she slid them from his hips and down his legs. Kicking them aside, he stepped forward and took her into his arms. The feel of her soft breasts crushed to his chest, her hardened nipples pressing into his skin, had his body feeling as if he'd go up in flames.

A shaft of need knifed through him when she skimmed her hands over his back and down his flanks, but when her slender fingers found him, Jake felt as if the intensity of pleasure would knock his knees right out from under him. As she gently measured his length and girth, he leaned down to capture one of her puckered nipples between his lips and worried it with butterfly flicks of his tongue.

Her soft moan was his reward and raising his head, he kissed her smooth cheek. "I think we'd better get into bed, honey. Otherwise, I'm not sure I'll have enough strength left to get there."

When she turned toward the bed, he reached into the night stand drawer to remove a small foil packet, then placing it under his pillow, stretched out beside her. Gathering her to him, he covered her mouth with his and let his kiss tell her how much the moment meant to him, how much he wanted her.

He'd never wanted to please a woman as much as he wanted to please Heather. "Honey, I'd like to take this slow, but I'm not entirely certain that's an option," he said hoarsely.

Heather gave him a look that sent liquid fire rushing through his veins as she wrapped her arms around his neck. "And I've wanted you just as much, Jake."

He'd been positive that she was experiencing the same desire, but having her confirm his assumption caused a fever within him that threatened to send him up in a blaze. Kissing her parted lips, he brought his hand up to cup her breast and tease the beaded tip.

When he took her nipple into his mouth, then sucked on it gently, a tiny moan escaped her lips and running her fingers through his hair, she held him to her. "That feels so…good."

Kissing his way down her smooth, flat stomach, Jake slid his hand along her side to her hip, then down her slender thigh to her knee. She shivered against him and he knew her excitement was building. He wanted to bring her to even greater heights and, trailing his fingers along the inner part of her thigh, teased the sensitive skin as he went.

"Jake, you're driving…me crazy," she softly gasped.

When he parted her and found her hot, wet and ready for him, he was the one feeling as if he might go insane. Just knowing that she needed him as much as he needed her sent blood racing through his veins and he had to use every ounce of his concentration to keep from losing the slender thread he still held on his control.

He wanted nothing more than to bury himself deep inside of her, to bring them both the completion they desired. He took a deep breath and forced himself to slow down. He was an accomplished lover and never failed to satisfy his partner. But it was more important to him than ever that he ensure Heather's pleasure above his own.

"P-please…Jake."

Apparently, she was feeling the same urgency because she suddenly moved to find his arousal, then taking him into her delicate hand stroked him intimately. A white-hot haze began to build deep within him and he had to fight with everything that was in him to keep from plunging over the edge.

"Just a moment, honey," he said, reaching for the packet beneath his pillow. Quickly rolling their protection into place, he nudged her knees apart and settling himself in the cradle of her hips, entered her with one smooth stroke.

Gritting his teeth at the mind-blowing tightness surrounding him, he leaned down to capture her lips with his as he slowly began to move within her. But the tension building between them was like a wild-fire, untamed and out of control. Each movement, each kiss, fanned the flame and drove them ever closer to being consumed by the passion.

When Heather suddenly arched up to meet him and he felt the immediate tightening around him, felt her feminine muscles cling to him, he deepened his strokes. He held her close and watched in awe as the ecstasy overtook her and she let go.

With his own release close, he moved into her again. He felt Heather suddenly tighten around him one more time and cry out his name. The mind-numbing realization that he'd brought her to a second release sent him over the edge. As he surged into her one final time, shock waves so strong they reverberated throughout his entire being shook him.

Easing to her side before he collapsed on top of her, he gathered Heather close and held her to him as they both tried to catch their breath. Shaken by the intensity of what they'd shared, Jake knew for certain that he'd never experienced anything as meaningful as their lovemaking. But even though he wasn't at all ready to try to put a name to what he was feeling, he wasn't fool enough to try to deny that it existed, either. And that should have made him nervous enough to jump out of his own skin. It was a mystery to him why it didn't.

"Are you all right?" he asked, kissing the top of her head where it rested on his shoulder.

"Mmm. That was incredible."

"I couldn't agree more." When she yawned and snuggled against him, he smiled and tightened his arms around her. "Why don't you get some sleep, honey? It's been a long day and the week has just started. We have about half a dozen more parties and receptions to attend before all of this is over."

"That many?"

"Unfortunately."

When she started to get up, he tightened his arms around her. "Where do you think you're going?"

She tilted her head up to look at him. "My room."

"I don't think so." He reached over to turn off the bedside lamp. "I want you right here."

"But—"

"I want to wake up with you tomorrow morning and make love again." He brushed her lips with his. "I can't do that if you're in one room and I'm in another."

She nibbled on her lower lip and he could tell she was waging an internal debate with herself. "Jake, I'm not sure this is such a good idea."

He knew she was afraid of getting in over her head. Hell, he was in uncharted waters himself.

"Please spend the night with me, honey," he pressed. "Then we'll take this one day at a time and see where it goes."

She stared at him for what seemed like forever before she finally nodded. "I'll stay tonight, but that's it. And when your family arrives in a few days, Mandy and I are going to move back into the carriage house."

"Why?"

"Because by my calculations, you're going to need our bedrooms to accommodate everyone."

"This suite is huge," he said, thinking fast. "We can move Mandy's crib in the sitting room and you can sleep with me."

She stubbornly shook her head. "I told you, I'll only stay with you tonight. And we will move back to the carriage house in a few days."

He could tell she wasn't going to concede the issue. But he didn't like the idea of not having her with him, in his house, in his bed.

"All right," he finally agreed.

Apparently satisfied that he'd given up, she laid her head on his shoulder and in no time he could tell that she'd drifted off to sleep.

As he lay there holding her and staring at the ceiling, determination filled him. Hickory Hills was her and Mandy's home and they belonged right where they were. And he was certain he could come up with some reason for them to stay in the house. All he had to do was find it.

# Seven

"Heather isn't gonna like this," Daily said, looking uncertain.

Jake gave the boy an encouraging smile as they carried the sofa from the carriage house and loaded it onto a truck. "You let me worry about Heather. Just make sure you don't drop your end of this thing."

After she, Clara and the baby had left to go into Louisville for lunch and shopping, Emerald had called, prompting him to enlist Daily's help in emptying out the carriage house. Heather was probably going to throw a fit about it, but once he explained everything, she'd surely understand. The place needed to be repainted and recarpeted, and it wouldn't hurt to have some of the furniture replaced. He'd intended to make some of the renovations for her anyway, just not quite this soon.

But when Emerald finally returned his call to tell him she was accepting his invitation to attend the race, she'd asked for downstairs rooms for herself and her assistant, and in doing so handed him the perfect excuse to keep Heather and Mandy in the house with him when the family descended upon them in a few days. Due to Emerald being somewhere in her mid-seventies and her assistant, Luther, being every bit as old, she'd reminded him that climbing the staircase in the mansion might not be a good idea for them. That's when he'd come to the conclusion that the one-level carriage house was the perfect solution.

"How long before the painters get here?" Daily asked, interrupting his thoughts.

As they turned to go back inside for the last pieces of furniture, Jake checked his watch. "They should be here anytime. We'd better get the rest of this stuff loaded on the truck and take it to the storage unit, so the men can get started." He was having to pay double the normal rate to get everything done in time. But in the end, it was going to be well worth it.

Daily looked almost as nervous as the night he'd tried to sneak out to see his girlfriend. "Have you figured out how you're going to keep Heather from finding out what's going on until everything's finished?"

"I'm not." Jake laughed at the boy's horrified expression.

"She's gonna kill both of us when she finds out," Daily said, shaking his head. "It's been nice knowing you."

"Don't worry. I'll take the heat with Heather," Jake assured. "You're just doing what I asked you to do."

An hour later, he and Daily had the carriage house emptied and the furniture unloaded into the storage unit. The painting crew had just finished taping the woodwork and were laying down drop cloths when Heather, Clara and the baby drove up in Heather's old sedan. "Jake, what's going on?" she asked when she got out of the car.

"I'm having the place renovated," he answered, hoping her reaction wasn't going to be as dire as Daily had predicted.

"What do you mean by that?" she demanded, her voice reflecting her displeasure.

"I'm having it painted and recarpeted."

She propped both fists on her shapely hips. "What did you do with my furniture and all of my things?"

"I stored the furniture until the work is finished and put all of your personal effects in your room in the mansion." He'd contemplated moving them to his room, but abandoned that idea after some careful thought. He'd reasoned that she'd be irritated enough that her plans to move back into the carriage house had to be changed, and there was no sense adding more fuel to that particular fire.

"You can't do this, Jake." Her voice shook with anger as she walked up to stand toe to toe with him. "I liked everything the way it was."

"You're on your own, dude," Daily said, taking off down the path toward the stables as if the hounds of hell chased him.

"I'll go ahead and take Mandy into the house," Clara offered as she quickly moved to get the baby out of the car seat.

Jake waited until Clara crossed the patio and entered the house with Mandy before he turned his full attention on Heather. If he was going to get himself out of the hole he'd dug with her, he figured he'd better do some fast talking.

"Before you become too upset, let me explain."

She folded her arms beneath her breasts. If looks could kill, he figured he'd be a dead man in nothing flat. "This had better be good."

"I received a call from my paternal grandmother this morning. She's going to join the rest of the family here for the race this weekend."

"And?"

"She and her assistant are both elderly." He wasn't about to tell her that Emerald and Luther were two of the spryest septuagenarians he'd ever met and that he strongly suspected Emerald's request was another ploy to control the situation. "There isn't an elevator in the mansion and I don't think it's a good idea for them to climb the stairs to get to their rooms. At their ages, a fall could be disastrous."

He could tell by her sudden frown that she was giving his reasoning consideration. "I can understand your concerns, but you should have discussed this with me first, instead of taking it upon yourself to start changing things." She pointed to the front door of the carriage house. "That's my home and I should have something to say about what goes on with it. You had no right to get rid of my furniture."

Reaching out, he pulled her into his arms. "Honey, this whole farm is your home. And your furniture will be moved back in as soon as the work is done. I promise the only thing different will be the color of the walls and carpet."

He lowered his head and kissed her until they both gasped for air. "If you decide later to move back into the carriage house, won't it be nice to have those things already done?"

"There's still a problem of not having enough bedrooms in the house when your family arrives."

"I'll have it all worked out by the time they get here." He was just glad she wasn't still glaring daggers at him. "Now, let's go into the house so you can show me the hat you bought for the race and explain to me why all of the women wear them."

\* \* \*

After dinner, Heather sorted through the boxes Jake had moved from the carriage house. She should have anticipated him finding a way to get her to stay in the mansion while his family visited. But she had to admit he did have a valid reason. There was no way she'd subject two elderly people to the perils of climbing all of those steps. She'd never forgive herself if one of them fell and was seriously injured.

"What are you doing in here, honey?" Jake asked from the door.

"I'm trying to organize and find a place to put everything until after your family leaves and Mandy and I can move back into the carriage house," she answered without looking up.

He walked over to sit on the bed beside her. "I meant it when I told you that I want you and Mandy to feel free to live in the mansion whether I'm here or not."

She sighed heavily. "Do we have to go over this again? It doesn't belong to me and I wouldn't feel right—"

"We'll cross that bridge when the time comes," he interrupted. "Right now, I have something I want you to see."

"This is the only free evening we've had in the past few days and I'd really like to relax." When she'd discovered they didn't have a reception to attend, she'd looked forward to a quiet, uneventful night.

Taking her hand, he pulled her to her feet. "Trust me, you're going to like this."

She allowed him to lead her down the hallway to the stairs. "Let's get this over with. I have a date with the Jacuzzi a little later."

His grin caused her to feel warm all over. "Want company? I'll wash your back if you'll wash mine."

The thought of being in the bubbling water with him caused a delightful fluttering in the pit of her stomach.

"We'll talk about it later." She stopped as he led her toward the front door. "I forgot the baby monitor."

"Don't worry about Mandy," he said, opening the door. "I asked Clara to watch her." He covered her eyes with his hand. "Now, follow me."

"But she has been babysitting so much the past few days." She let him lead her out onto the veranda. "I hate to take advantage of her."

"Clara volunteered." She could hear the smile in his voice as he helped her down the steps. "I think she knows we both need some downtime. Besides, she told me the other day that it's a lot easier to grand-mother a baby than a teenager."

Nodding, Heather laughed. "I've seen Daily turn as red as a beet when she kisses his cheek, whereas Mandy loves it."

"Are you ready for the surprise?"

"I suppose so." She couldn't imagine why he was being so secretive.

He removed his hand. A shiny royal-blue minivan with the farm logo sat in the driveway. "What do you think?"

"Who does that belong to?" she asked cautiously.

"The farm. But it's primarily for your use."

She turned to stare at him. "Why?"

He pulled her along as he circled the car and opened the sliding side door. "I saw how cramped the backseat of your car is with Mandy's car seat, and you can definitely use the room. Besides, it's not fair for you to drive your car for the farm business."

He handed her a set of keys. "Try it out."

She bit her lower lip. It was such a pretty car and would save her from having to put a lot more miles on her aging Taurus. "I'll only use it to go to meetings and to pick up things for the farm."

"Honey, I want you to feel free to use it whenever you like. I'd feel better if you and Mandy were in this than a car that could break down and strand you somewhere." He urged her to get behind the wheel, then walked around to close the side door. But before he slid it shut, Nemo jumped in and sat down on the bench seat in the back. "What the hell?"

"He likes to go for rides," she said, laughing.

Jake patted the big dog's head, then, closing the

door, got into the passenger seat. "I guess we'll take Nemo for a ride."

By the time they drove several miles down the road and back to the mansion, Heather had fallen in love with the new car. "This is wonderful," she said when she parked it and they coaxed Nemo out of the backseat.

"I'm glad you like it," he said, smiling warmly as he picked up a clump of dog hair from the leather seat, then, tossing it to the ground, closed the door. "I'll install a car seat tomorrow and you'll be good to go."

As they walked hand in hand into the house, she started to go back upstairs, but he stopped her. "Where do you think you're going? The evening has just started."

"What do you have up your sleeve this time?" she asked, smiling.

Leading her into the den, he motioned for her to sit on the sectional couch in front of a large flat-panel television. As she sank into the plush cushions, she noticed a bowl of popcorn and a couple of soft drinks on the coffee table.

"I thought we could watch a movie together," he said, sitting beside her. He picked up a remote control, pushed a button to start the movie, then put his arms around her shoulder and pulled her close. "We've been on the go so much lately, I figured it might be a good way to relax."

Settling back into his embrace, Heather munched on popcorn and watched the comedy he'd selected for them. She briefly wondered if Jake felt as happy and content as she did. This was her idea of the perfect evening, but she wasn't sure about him. He seemed to be enjoying the quiet evening at home. But he could very well just be marking time until he could get back to the fast-paced lifestyle he led in Los Angeles. After all, he was used to going out every night and partying until the wee hours of the morning.

"What's running through that head of yours?" he asked, startling her. He switched off the television.

"Why do you ask?"

"Because you look pensive and you're not paying attention to the movie." He used his index finger to brush a strand of hair from her cheek. "Otherwise, you would have laughed. Especially at that last part."

She stared at him for several seconds before she voiced her thoughts. "I was just wondering if you're bored yet."

He frowned. "Where did that come from?"

Shrugging one shoulder, she met his confused gaze. "You've been here a week and other than the sedate receptions and the ball last night, you haven't gone out to any of the clubs. And you've had more than enough time after you brought me home to go back out. But you didn't. I would have thought by now you'd be climbing the walls."

"Honey, I haven't missed that scene one time since I've been here." He looked thoughtful as if he couldn't quite believe it himself. "In fact, I don't find the idea of going clubbing the least bit appealing."

"Are you feeling all right?" she asked before she could stop herself.

He unbuttoned his shirt, then, taking her hand in his, placed it on his bare chest. "You tell me."

Her pulse sped up. "I think you feel pretty good. Wonderful actually."

Pulling her onto his lap, he cradled her to him as he tugged her shirt from her jeans and slipped his hand under the hem. When he cupped her breast, he rested his forehead against hers. "You feel pretty awesome yourself."

A delicious warmth began to flow through her veins and she closed her eyes as she lost herself to the sensation of his hand on her sensitive skin. Was it possible that he really didn't miss his old lifestyle? Or when the first opportunity presented itself, would he revert to his old ways?

Jake covered her mouth with his and she gave up all speculation. She didn't want to think about what tomorrow would bring. At the moment, she was in his arms and that was all that mattered.

"Let's go upstairs, honey," he said, ending the kiss. "I think your suggestion about our having a date with the Jacuzzi is an excellent idea."

Putting her arms around his shoulders, she smiled. "I thought that was *my* date."

His mischievous grin caused her heart to skip a beat. "Do you mind if I make it *ours?*"

"Not at all."

When he set her on her feet and stood, she didn't think twice about placing her hand in his and walking out of the den and up the stairs. As they entered the master bedroom, he ushered her into the sitting area and over to one of the chairs.

"Stay right here," he said a moment before he disappeared into the bathroom. A couple of minutes later, he walked back into the room and, smiling, leaned down to kiss the tip of her nose. "Come with me, Heather. I have a surprise for you."

Doing as he requested, when he led her into the bathroom, she couldn't believe her eyes. The flicker of white candles in all shapes and sizes lit the otherwise dark room and the filled bathtub was already bubbling.

"When did you do this? There wasn't enough time—"

"I set the candles out and filled the tub earlier. The thermostat kept it warm for us." He took her into his arms. "I just lit the candles."

She wrapped her arms around him and laid her head against his chest. "This is perfect. Thank you."

"Let's get undressed and see if it's as relaxing as it looks," he suggested.

Taking turns removing each other's clothes, Jake stepped into the Jacuzzi and eased her between his thighs. The feel of his body against hers when he pulled her back to lie against him sent electricity skipping over every cell in her being.

"This feels so good," he said as he tightened his arms around her.

"Yes, it does." She blissfully closed her eyes. "The water is just right."

His low chuckle caused goose bumps to shimmer over her. "I wasn't talking about the water." A shiver of excitement coursed through her when he kissed her shoulder at the same time his hands covered her breasts. "Tonight is all for you, honey. I'm going to love you so well that there won't be a doubt left in your mind how much I desire you."

The sound of his deep baritone promising a night of passion and the feel of his rapidly hardening body against her backside caused her to feel as if she never wanted to be anywhere else but in his arms. And that's when it hit her. She'd told herself that it wasn't happening and tried her best not to do it, but she'd fallen hopelessly in love with him.

If she'd had the chance, she might have been frightened beyond words. There was a very real possibility that she would get hurt again. But Jake didn't give her the opportunity. His hands were moving over her body with precision care and robbed her of all thought.

When he slid his palm down her abdomen to the apex of her thighs, then gently parted her to stroke the tiny nub nestled within, Heather felt as if a spark ignited in her soul. The intensity of the sensations coursing through her caused her body to hum with a need stronger than anything she had ever known.

"Jake, please."

"What do you want, Heather?"

"Y-you."

She turned her head to look over her shoulder at him. "Please make love to me."

His deep groan vibrated against her back. "Turn around, honey."

When she did as he commanded and straddled his thighs, he lifted up to meet her and entered her in one smooth motion. The feel of his hard body nestled inside of her and the hunger darkening his blue eyes stole her breath.

She watched him tightly close his eyes as he struggled for control and she knew his need was as great as hers. Without hesitation she wrapped her arms around his neck and slowly moved against him. His eyes immediately snapped open and, placing his hands on her hips, he helped her set a steady pace.

Feeling more cherished than she had in her entire life, she bit her lower lip to keep from crying out at the intensity of emotions swirling through her. She loved Jake with all of her heart and soul.

As the knowledge filled her, an undeniable tension built inside of her and she rapidly began to climb toward the peak. Jake must have sensed her readiness and, deepening his thrusts, he sent her over the edge. As her body clung to his, waves of pleasure flowed through her and almost immediately she felt him tense, then give in to the force of his own climax. His tremors rocked them both and she held him close as they rode out the storm together.

When they slowly drifted back to reality, Jake's heart suddenly pounded so hard against his ribs, he wasn't entirely certain it wouldn't jump out of his chest. "Dammit all to hell."

"What's wrong?" Heather asked, clearly startled by his outburst.

He set her away from him and moved to get out of the Jacuzzi. "I wanted you so much, I didn't even consider protection."

She smiled. "Oh, that."

Why was she taking it so lightly? They already had one baby they hadn't planned. And although he loved Mandy more than life itself, he didn't think having another was going to help an already complicated situation.

"Let's get out of here and dry off," he said, wondering if he'd lost his mind. As he got out of the bathtub, he handed her a plush towel, then dried himself off with another.

There was no question about it. He didn't want to make her pregnant again. Hell, he didn't know if he was a good father to one child yet, let alone two.

He shook his head in an attempt to clear it. There hadn't been one time in his life that he'd failed to use protection. Even as a teenager, he'd been conscious of the implications and responsibilities attached to an unplanned pregnancy.

"Jake, are you listening to me?" she asked, wrapping the towel around her.

He'd been so distracted, he hadn't realized she was trying to talk to him. Securing the towel at his waist, he motioned toward the door. "Let's go into the bedroom, honey. We need to talk."

"But I'm trying to tell you—"

He placed his index finger to her lips. "Not until I've had my say."

She looked thoughtful for a moment before she nodded and, walking into the bedroom, sat down on the side of the bed. "I'm listening."

Unable to stand still, he paced back and forth in front of her. "There's no excuse for my forgetting to protect you." He stopped and ran his hand over the tension building at the base of his neck. "But I want you to know that if you do get pregnant because of my carelessness, I'll be there this time." He knelt in front of her and took her hands in his. "I promise you won't have to go through everything alone like you did when you were pregnant with Mandy. This time I'll know, and I give you my word that I'll be there for you, Heather."

"Are you finished?"

He couldn't believe her lack of concern. Did she want to become pregnant again?

Nodding, he drew in a deep breath. "Yes, I think that about covers it."

"You can stop worrying. I'm not going to get pregnant." She shrugged one bare shoulder. "There was an issue of my being regular after Mandy was born, so the doctor put me on the Pill."

Instead of the relief he should have felt, disappointment settled in the pit of his belly. Had he really wanted to make her pregnant again? Had he lost what little sense he had left?

Of course not. The thought was ludicrous. But he couldn't seem to chase away the let-down feeling that accompanied her announcement.

"Why didn't you tell me?" he asked.

"The subject never came up. And besides, it really wasn't any of your business."

She was right, of course. But what he couldn't understand was why he wanted it to be.

Reaching out, she touched his cheeks with her soft hand, then leaned forward and gave him a kiss so sweet it robbed him of breath. "You wouldn't have gotten so worked up if you'd only let me explain. You really could use some work on your listening skills, Mr. Garnier."

Two hours later, after making love to Heather again, Jake held her close as she slept and thought about his uncharacteristic emotions. Not quite two weeks ago, he'd been a carefree, commitment-shy bachelor with nothing more on his mind than paying a visit to his newly acquired horse farm, sticking around for the big race, and then he was supposed to be back on the road to L.A. But all that had changed with the discovery that he'd not only found the one woman he'd regretted not staying in touch with but also that she'd had his baby.

Why did he all of a sudden want all of the things he'd spent most of his adult life trying to avoid?

Tightening his arms around her, he pulled her close and tried to relax. But as sleep began to overtake him, Jake couldn't help but feel that he was walking a fine line. And once crossed there would be no going back.

"How's my little angel?" Heather asked as she picked the baby up from the crib. "Did you have a good nap?"

Mandy's happy grin as Heather changed her diaper revealed a small white place on her lower gum.

"Your tooth has broken through." Kissing her daughter's soft cheek, Heather picked her up from the changing table and walked out of her bedroom toward the stairs. "We'll have to find your daddy and show him. He's been worried about when it was finally going to stop bothering you."

Shortly after awakening to find herself alone in Jake's bed that morning, she'd gone in search of him and found that he had moved the crib into the room she'd been using. He'd explained that with his grandmother and her assistant staying in the newly decorated carriage house there would be plenty of rooms for everyone when they descended on them later in the day.

Hearing voices when she reached the bottom of the steps, she crossed the foyer and, entering the den, found several people taking their turns hugging Jake. It appeared that his family had arrived.

"Heather, I'd like you to meet the clan," Jake said when he noticed her standing just inside the door. Walking over, he lifted Mandy onto his arm and put his other arm around her shoulders. "This is my daughter, Mandy, and her mother, Heather."

"Please let me hold her," his sister, Arielle, said reaching for Mandy. Almost six months pregnant, she and her husband, Zach, had just learned they were expecting twin boys. "She's absolutely adorable. And she looks just like you, Jake."

As everyone greeted her and made a fuss over the baby, a bittersweet feeling filled her chest at the pride in Jake's voice. She only wished he could love her half as much as he did their baby.

When he finished making the introductions, Heather couldn't help but notice how much Jake and his half brothers were alike. All of them were quite tall, had the same athletic build and bore a strong facial resemblance. They even shared some of the same mannerisms. When his brother Hunter O'Banyon talked about the stress of being an air medevac pilot, he ran his hand over the back of his neck, which Jake had a habit of doing, too.

"Where's your twin and his wife?" she asked, noticing their absence.

"Haley had a doctor's appointment," Jake answered. "Luke said they'd meet us at Churchill Downs before the race tomorrow."

"Heather, I hear you're the one in charge of the winning horse," Nick Daniels said. "Jake told us you raised him from a colt."

Smiling, she nodded at the rancher from Wyoming. "Actually, I was responsible for choosing his bloodlines as well as helping the mare foal when the vet couldn't get here in time."

"Hang on to her, Jake," Nick advised. He put his arm around his pretty wife, Cheyenne. "Take it from me. You can't go wrong with a woman who knows her horses."

"I'll remember that," Jake said, smiling.

"Heather, do you have time to go shopping with us?" Caleb Walker's wife, Alyssa, asked. "I've heard that it's a tradition for all of the women to wear a hat to the race."

"I got a new one a couple of days ago and I'd be more than happy to take all of you to the shop where I bought it," Heather offered. "They have a great selection, in all colors and styles."

Callie O'Banyon sighed. "A shopping trip without little ones in tow sounds like heaven."

"By the way, where are your children?" Jake asked.

Caleb chuckled as he pointed to his brothers. "We all decided to leave them with the babysitters and enjoy spending a little alone time with our wives."

"If everyone's agreeable on the shopping, we could go right after I take a nap," Arielle suggested, yawning. She handed Mandy to Alyssa, then with her husband's help rose to her feet. "Could you tell me where our room is, Jake?"

"I'll be happy to show you where you'll be staying," Heather spoke up, earning a warm smile from Jake.

When they climbed the stairs and Heather showed the pretty young woman where she and her husband, Zach, would be sleeping during their stay at Hickory Hills, Arielle motioned for Heather to follow her into the room. "Are you up for some girl talk before I crash?"

Heather liked all of Jake's brothers and sisters-in-law, but there was something about Arielle that told

Heather if given the chance they would become very good friends. "Of course."

Lowering herself to the side of the bed, Arielle smiled. "I just wanted you to know how thrilled I am that someone has finally tamed Jake. I couldn't be happier for both of you."

Heather frowned. "I think you must have gotten the wrong impression. Jake and I are just—"

"Don't tell me you're just friends," Arielle interrupted. "I've seen the way my brother looks at you and there's a lot more to the way he feels about you than friendship."

Heather wasn't quite sure what to say. She wasn't going to lie to the woman. But she wasn't certain there was anything more going on for Jake than a strong attraction and undeniable desire.

"It's…complicated," she finally said, settling on the truth. Whatever was going on between them was going to take some time to sort out. They still hadn't discussed how they were going to handle raising Mandy together with so much distance between their residences. Jake had talked about going back to Los Angeles and leaving her and Mandy the run of the farm, but that didn't mean the custody issue was settled. He could still come up with demands for equal time.

Arielle placed her hand over Heather's. "You love him, don't you?"

She didn't even think to hesitate. "Yes."

"Trust me, Jake may not realize it yet, but he's in love with you, too," Arielle said, smiling. "I've never seen him like this. He can't keep his eyes off of you."

"It's not like he has much to choose from here," Heather said dryly. "Besides the housekeeper, Clara Buchanan, who's sixty if she's a day, I'm the only other woman here at Hickory Hills."

Arielle laughed. "How many times has he been out since he's been here?"

"Other than the receptions and ball we've had to attend, he hasn't," she admitted.

"I rest my case." Arielle hid a yawn behind her hand. "I know my brother. If he didn't have some very strong feelings for you, he would have been out every night."

"I wish you were right, but—"

"I am." The young woman yawned again. "Now, why don't you go downstairs and get to know the others while I take my nap. When I get up we'll all go shopping and buy some wildly expensive hats we'll probably never wear after the race tomorrow."

Heather gave Arielle a hug, then walked out into the hall and quietly pulled the door shut behind her. She'd give almost anything for Jake's sister to be right. But she couldn't trust that Jake had changed for good. Before coming to Kentucky, he'd been perfectly content being the irresponsible bachelor with no children and no commitments. And once he was back in his element in Los Angeles, around friends who enjoyed partying all the time, he just might find that he'd missed that nonstop excitement and revert to his old ways.

# Eight

"Heather, I'd like for you to meet my paternal grandmother, Emerald Larson," Jake said, wondering how she'd take the news that he was the grandson of one of the richest women in the world.

The one thing that Emerald had respected and taken great pains to protect was her grandchildren's right to privacy. She left it entirely up to them when and to whom they revealed the relationship. And as if by unspoken agreement, all six of them had been discreet and managed to keep the news fairly quiet.

As he watched, Heather's aqua eyes widened a moment before she recovered and shook Emerald's hand. "It's nice to meet you, Mrs. Larson."

"I see Jake has taken his cue from the rest of my

grandchildren," Emerald said, patting Heather's cheek. "Don't worry, dear. None of the others revealed my identity until they had to, either."

"If you'll excuse me, I was just on my way to the paddock to see if Tony has everything under control," Heather said, rising from her seat.

As she started past him, Jake caught her hand in his. "Will you be back in time for the race?"

Her smile lit the darkest corners of his soul. "Absolutely. I wouldn't miss this for anything."

"Where's your assistant?" he asked Emerald as he watched Heather disappear into the crowd.

Since Emerald never went anywhere without the distinguished-looking gentleman, Jake knew he couldn't be too far away. He just hoped he didn't have to go looking for Luther in the sea of people. Churchill Downs had a record crowd and he'd probably never find the poor old guy.

"Luther is placing a small wager for me on your horse, Jake," Emerald said as she found a seat in the box section he'd reserved for the family to watch the race.

Unless she'd changed her ways, Emerald never did anything on a small scale. No telling how much she'd had Luther put down on Stormy Dancer. But it wasn't as if she couldn't afford it. She could probably buy the entire race track with all of the horses and not even scratch the surface of her bank account.

"This is such a festive atmosphere," she said,

looking genuinely excited. "And I love that all of the ladies have such decorative hats." She touched the brim of her own elaborate headwear. "I think it's sad that these aren't called for on more occasions. I can remember a time when all the women wore hats for every occasion."

Jake paid little attention to what she was saying as he scanned the crowd for Emerald's assistant, Luther Freemont. When he finally spotted him, Jake breathed a sigh of relief. The man was slowly making his way through the crowd to the box section with a mint julep in each hand and a bet slip sticking out of the breast pocket of his suit.

"Mr. Garnier." Luther nodded a greeting in his usually stiff manner, then handed one of the glasses to Emerald. "Your julep, madam."

"Thank you, Luther." Emerald patted the seat beside her and the man lowered himself into it. "I'm so glad we're right here in front of the finish line. We'll be able to see Jake's horse win."

As the bugler played the call to race, his brothers and their wives began to file into the box. Jake checked his watch. Where the hell was Heather? She should have been back from checking on Dancer down at the paddock by now.

Just as the horses began their parade past the grandstand on their way to the starting gate, he saw her hurrying up the steps. "Was everything all right?" he asked when she reached him.

"Dancer was a little more skittish than usual," she said, sitting down beside him. "Thoroughbreds are high-strung by nature—he can sense this is the race of his life."

"Which one is Stormy Dancer?" Caleb asked from behind them.

"That's Dancer," Heather spoke up, pointing to one of the bays. "Our silks are red and blue with a white stripe cutting diagonally across the jockey's chest. When they're running along the back stretch or packed up, look for the colors and you'll be able to keep track of him during the race."

"Thanks for the tip," Caleb said, picking up a set of binoculars.

"There's a lot to remember in this business," Luke said, laughing as he sat down on the other side of Jake.

"Tell me about it, bro." Glancing at his twin, he felt as if he looked into a mirror. Lowering his voice, he admitted, "I couldn't have gotten through these past couple of weeks without Heather. Every time a question was asked about Dancer or his training, she'd tell the reporters and sportscasters what they needed to know."

Luke looked thoughtful. "When's the wedding?"

"How many mint juleps have you had?" Irritated, Jake shook his head. "If I were you, I'd lay off for a while."

Luke shrugged. "Still in denial, huh?"

Before he could tell his brother to mind his own damned business, they started loading the horses into the starting gate and everyone jumped to their feet. As soon as the last horse was guided into place, the front of the chutes flew open at the same time the announcer shouted, "They're off."

The roar of the crowd made it impossible to be heard, and when the horses raced past the grandstand, Heather grabbed his hand and squeezed it until his fingers went numb. He barely noticed. He was too busy watching her. Her cheeks had colored a pretty pink and he didn't think he'd ever seen her look more breathtaking. With sudden insight, he realized that he'd underestimated how much it would mean to her if the horse she'd raised won. She'd chosen his bloodlines, overseen his development and this race was her validation—the culmination of her work.

The horses entered the backstretch and Jake noticed that the sheikh's horse was way out in front, just as Heather said he would be. Picking up the binoculars he'd brought with him, Jake searched for Dancer and found him in the middle of the pack. As they rounded the turn and headed for the home stretch, their jockey must have turned Dancer loose because he suddenly shot to the outside and made his way to the front. And as Heather predicted, the sheikh's horse started slipping back into the pack and Dancer took over the lead. By the time he sprinted across the finish line he was five or six lengths ahead of his nearest challenger and there was no doubt he'd won the race.

"We won!"

With enough adrenaline flowing through his veins to lift a freight train, Jake caught Heather up in his arms and kissed her like a soldier returning from war. He knew his level of elation had nothing to do with their horse winning and everything to do with the relief that she hadn't been disappointed with the results of the race.

When he set her on her feet, she grabbed his hand. "We need to get down to the track. After Miguel weighs in with the saddle, they'll want you in the winner's circle."

Jake shook his head. "They want *us* in the winner's circle, honey. I may be the owner on paper, but Dancer has always been your horse and always will be."

Tears filled her eyes and she raised up on tiptoes to lightly kiss his cheek. "Thank you, Jake. That means a lot to me."

After posing for endless pictures and helping Jake get through the required interviews with the media, Heather called Clara to check on Mandy. Then, leaving orders with Tony to give Dancer an extra scoop of oats to celebrate, she joined Jake and his family for an elaborate dinner at the hotel where the Southern Oaks Ball had been held.

Once their waiter had popped the cork on a bottle of outrageously expensive champagne, Jake stood up and raised his glass. "To Heather, her excellent instincts and expertise. Today was the culmination of your hard work and the realization of a dream. May Dancer be the first of many winners under your expert management."

As everyone added their congratulations, Jake sat back down beside her. "Thank you," she whispered, blinking back tears. His recognition of her accomplishment meant more to her than he'd probably ever know.

"You deserve all of the credit and accolades for the outcome of today's race, honey." His hand found hers beneath the table and he gave it a gentle squeeze. "And I couldn't be happier for you."

When the waiter served the main course, conversation turned to catching up on what was going on in the various lives of Jake's siblings, and Heather found it heartwarming that in spite of their unconventional relationship, they'd all become good friends.

"What's up next for you, Jake?" Hunter asked. "Any more big races on the horizon?"

"I'm leaving that up to Heather," he answered. "I called a Realtor yesterday to put my condo on the market and have her find a house along the beach in Malibu for me."

As the group left the private dining room and entered the Grand Ballroom for the victory party,

Heather didn't have time to dwell on what Jake might have planned as she noticed several celebrities milling around the bar. All of them had notorious reputations for partying and she couldn't help but wonder if some of them were Jake's friends.

When a singer started singing the song they'd danced to at the ball, Jake turned to her, smiling. "I think they're playing our song, Heather." Leading her out onto the dance floor, he wrapped his arms around her. "Are you happy, honey?"

She stared up at the man she loved with all of her heart. "And you?"

"Let's see. Our horse won the Classic. The family all made it for the big race. I have a sweet baby daughter with a new tooth who loves to throw baby food at me. And you're in my arms." He brushed his lips over hers. "What more could a man ask for?"

She wanted to believe that all of that would be enough for him. Unfortunately, she knew it wasn't. If he'd already started looking for a house along the beach in Malibu, where she was certain several of his acquaintances had property, he wasn't considering leaving the wilder side of life behind.

The song ended and the orchestra immediately began to play the other tune they'd danced to. Looking up into his cobalt eyes, she blinked back tears. "You arranged for those songs to be played back to back, didn't you?"

His smile made her feel warm all over in spite of

the disappointment filling her. "They will always remind me of you and a very special night we spent together." He tenderly kissed her forehead. "You're so beautiful and I want you so much right now."

She loved the way his body felt against hers. "I want you, too. But—"

"I know. You don't have to say it." He shook his head. "Do you think I can charter a jet to take my family all back to their homes tonight?"

She shook her head. "I don't think that would be a good idea."

"I do."

When the music stopped and he led her off the dance floor, her earlier speculation was answered about the celebrities in attendance being his friends when a tall, dark-haired man she recognized as one of Hollywood's baddest bad boys walked toward them. "Jake Garnier, I heard you owned the horse that won today. I hoped you'd stop by this evening." The man grinned from ear to ear, showing off a mouthful of capped teeth. "Now I know this little bash is going to rock."

"What are you doing here, Cameron?" Jake asked, smiling at his friend.

"One of the actresses in my latest film is part owner in one of the nags that ran in the big race and she asked me to come along with her to watch." The conspiratorial wink he gave Jake set Heather's teeth on edge. "You know me. If a woman asks, I'm always up to the challenge." Turning his attention her way, the man's grin evolved into an outright leer. "And who do we have here?"

She felt the arm Jake had draped around her waist, stiffen. "Heather McGwire, this is the infamous Cameron Strombeck."

"Jake!" a tall willowy redhead called as she made her way across the dance floor toward them. "Congratulations. I'll bet you'll be out all night. Be sure and save a dance for me, darling."

As the celebrities continued to gravitate toward them, Heather felt increasingly more uncomfortable. It appeared that instead of having to go back home to pick up his life where it left off, Los Angeles had come to him.

"I think I'll join your family," she said, slipping from his arm before he could stop her.

She walked over to the table where the women were gathered as they waited for their husbands to return with their drinks and sank into an empty chair beside Arielle. "I hope you don't mind my joining you."

"Not at all," Callie O'Banyon said, smiling warmly.

"You and Jake looked amazing out there on the dance floor." Arielle reached over to hug her. "Congratulations, I'm so happy for you."

"Thank you. Dancer's win was definitely exciting." She knew that wasn't what the woman meant, but it was easier to change the subject than to accept good wishes for something that was never going to happen.

When the orchestra started playing again, the volume made conversation impossible and they all fell silent. Heather glanced at Jake several times and her heart broke a little more each time. He looked as if he was having the time of his life with his friends from Tinseltown. As she watched, the redhead melted against him on the dance floor. He didn't seem to mind in the least.

"I hope you don't mind but I think I'll call it a night," she said, rising to her feet.

"Heather, wait," Arielle said, placing a hand on her arm to stop her.

"I'm…um, really pretty tired. I'll see you all in the morning." She had to get out of there before she humiliated herself by dissolving into a torrent of tears. She'd done the very thing that she'd told herself she couldn't let happen. She'd started to believe that Jake might be content staying with her and Mandy. But she knew now that wasn't going to happen. He would soon be leaving Hickory Hills to return to his life in L.A. and the sooner she accepted that, the better off she'd be.

Hurrying across the hotel lobby, when she stepped out onto the sidewalk, she found Mrs. Larson and her assistant waiting on their limousine. "What's wrong, dear?" Mrs. Larson asked, clearly concerned.

Heather forced a smile. "It's been a full day and I'm going back to Hickory Hills before I collapse."

"Would you like to ride with us?" Mrs. Larson offered. "It's past our bedtime and we'd like to get a good night's sleep before we fly back to Wichita tomorrow."

"I would appreciate it. Thank you."

She'd intended to get a cab, but she was going to have to watch her money for a while. There was no way she could continue working for Jake after what she'd just witnessed. Effective the first thing tomorrow morning she was going to resign her position as farm manager and find employment elsewhere.

"Back off, Lila," Jake demanded, setting the woman away from him. Aside from the fact that he wanted nothing to do with the woman, he didn't want Heather getting the wrong idea.

"I thought you'd be open to having a little fun for old times." Her expression turned to a pout that he was certain she'd practiced for years. He couldn't for the life of him remember why he'd ever found her attractive.

"I'm with someone else. Besides, if you'll remember, that ship sailed a long time ago. We went out a total of three times. You've got to move on."

Her lips curled into what could only be described as a snarl. "You don't know what you're missing."

"Oh, I think I do." He started to walk away, then

turned back. "And don't worry. I'm sure you'll find someone to help you have a *good time* this evening. Have a nice life, Lila."

He glanced over at the table where his sister sat and breathed a sigh of relief. At least Heather hadn't been around to witness Lila's brazen move.

"Hey, Jake, would you like to go see what the clubs around here have to offer?" Cameron asked, stopping him half way across the room. "This is dull. We want a lot more action than what this horse crowd has to offer."

As he stared at the man, Jake couldn't believe he'd ever considered him a friend. A pleasure-seeker from the word go, Cameron Strombeck was about as shallow and self-absorbed as a human could possibly be. His disdain for the fine people of the racing industry—for people like Heather—grated on Jake's nerves as little else could.

"No, I'm fine right where I'm at. But you might want to check with Lila Dixon. I happen to know she's looking for a little excitement."

"Really? That could be interesting. I'll catch you when you get back to L.A., then," Cameron said, turning to find Lila. "Give me a call."

"Don't hold your breath on that happening," Jake muttered. Continuing on to the table where Arielle sat, he noticed that she looked ready to tear him in two. "What's wrong?"

"Sit."

"Where's Heather?"

"I said sit!" He didn't think he'd ever seen his sister look as determined as she did at that very moment.

"Where's Heather?" he repeated, desperately searching the ballroom for her. He saw his brothers and their wives on the dance floor and his brother-in-law, Zach, over by the bar. But Heather was nowhere in sight.

"She left." Arielle shook her head. "And I don't blame her. How could you do that to her, Jake? What were you thinking?"

"What the hell are you talking about? I didn't do anything."

When he started to get up, Arielle stopped him. "Stay right where you're at, big brother. I have something to ask you."

"It's going to have to wait, Arielle. I need to find Heather."

"You and Luke have made me listen to both of you all of my life, now you're going to hear what I have to say." He'd never known his sister to be this upset with him.

"Could you make it quick?" he asked impatiently. "I've got to get to Heather and find out why she left."

Arielle looked thoughtful a moment. "She's extremely important to you, isn't she, Jake?"

"Yes."

"You love her, don't you?" Arielle pressed.

"I wouldn't go that far," he said stubbornly. He knew he had deep feelings for Heather, but he wasn't comfortable with the word *love*.

"Oh, Jake." Arielle's voice softened as she reached out to put her arms around him. "You're frightened, aren't you?"

"That's ridiculous, Arielle." He hugged her back. "I can't think of one single thing I need to be scared of."

Leaning back, she smiled sadly. "How about losing Heather? Aren't you afraid of that?"

His chest tightened painfully at the thought of never holding her, loving her, again. "You don't understand, I..."

When his voice trailed off, his sister nodded. "That's exactly what's going to happen if you don't take the chance, Jake. I don't know what's holding you back, but whatever it is, you've got to let it go."

As he stared at his younger sister, he knew that she was right. He'd avoided making a commitment for fear of turning out to be as irresponsible as his father. But he was nothing like Owen Larsen and never would be.

No other woman incited the degree of passion in him or made him want her the way Heather did. And he'd never met any other woman who made him want to be a better person. Not until Heather.

Taking a deep breath, he rose to his feet and kissed

Arielle's cheek. "For a kid, you're pretty damned smart."

"What's going on?" Zach asked when he walked up to the table.

"I have to go find Heather and do some serious explaining," Jake answered, turning to leave.

"Stop by a sporting goods store first and get a set of knee pads," Zach called after him. "If Heather is anything like Arielle, you're going to need them when you're on your knees begging her to give you another chance."

After checking with Clara to see if she could watch Mandy for the rest of the evening, Heather barely managed to make it to her room upstairs and close the door before the tears she'd been holding in check spilled down her cheeks. How could she have let herself think there was a chance that Jake was different now than he'd been over a year ago? How could she have been so stupid?

Collapsing on the bed, she hugged one of the pillows. She should have known better than to think that he had changed. Jake was Jake. He couldn't be someone he wasn't, couldn't be the man she wanted him to be. Seeing him with his friends tonight and hearing his plans to buy a house in Malibu had been all the proof she needed to see that she and their daughter weren't enough for him.

She wasn't certain how long she lay there sobbing

against the pillow, but when she finally managed to stop crying, she gathered the scraps of her broken heart and got up. There were things she needed to do before she faced Jake tomorrow morning.

Going into the bathroom, she washed her face, then took off the evening gown she'd changed into for dinner and put on a pair of jeans and a T-shirt. She needed to pack her and her daughter's things and take them down to her old car, then draft her resignation.

As she opened the dresser drawers and started pulling out clothes, the sound of a car coming to a screeching halt in front of the mansion caused her to jump. Almost immediately she heard the front door bang back against the woodwork.

Hurrying to the top of the stairs to see what was going on, she stopped short at the sight of Jake, standing in the open doorway staring up at her.

"Heather, honey, we have to talk."

# Nine

"**I** don't *have* to do anything," Heather stated flatly.

She watched him release a frustrated breath. "Would you please come down here? I need to tell you something."

"Where are your friends?" she asked as she slowly descended the steps.

"Damned if I know and damned if I care." He closed the front door, then walked over to stand at the bottom of the staircase.

"I would have thought you'd be out celebrating with them," she said, drawing on every bit of strength and pride she could muster.

"That's one of the things we need to discuss."

When she descended the last step, he started to take her by the hand, but she sidestepped him. He stared at her for a moment before he motioned toward the study. "Please follow me."

"I don't really want to discuss anything right now, Jake." Did he think hearing that he was leaving her and Mandy would make everything all right?

She walked over to the fireplace and traced her finger along the frame of a snapshot that he'd had Clara or Daily take of himself holding their daughter. Just like the photograph, she was never going to be a part of the picture. The thought caused an ache so deep inside, she had to look away to keep from crying out.

When Jake put his hands on her shoulders to turn her to face him, she backed away from his touch. "Please don't."

"Heather, honey, you have to listen to me."

"You don't have to make excuses or explain," she said, surprised that her voice remained steady. "You're an adult. You can do as you please."

"But I'm going to tell you anyway," he interrupted. "Now, will you stop arguing with me and start listening?"

Sighing heavily, she walked over to sit in one of the chairs. "Let's get this over with. I have things to do."

He stared at her for several long seconds. "What do you have to do at this time of night?"

"I need to pack."

He folded his arms across his broad chest. "Are you going somewhere?"

"I suppose now is as good a time as any to tell you that I quit effective immediately." She had to pause before she could finish. "You'll have to find someone else to manage Hickory Hills and oversee your horses."

A dark scowl wrinkled his forehead. "You can't do that."

"Watch me." A sudden anger swept through her and she started to get up.

He quickly stepped forward to block her. "I won't let you quit and I don't want you leaving."

"You can't stop me," she said, settling back in the chair.

"Dammit, Heather, Hickory Hills is your and Mandy's home." He pulled another armchair over to sit in front of her. "You belong here."

"Not anymore, I don't." She glared at him. It was much easier to let her anger build than to give in to the misery of a broken heart. "You're going back to your life in L.A. and I'm staying here. But do you honestly think I want to be here when you bring a woman with you for your next visit? Or wait for you to return so that I can be a diversion while you're here?"

He shook his head. "That's not going to happen."

She watched him close his eyes as if garnering his patience. When he opened them, there was a determined spark in the cobalt depths.

"If you'd stuck around long enough you'd have seen me decline Cameron's invitation to go barhopping with him and a few others I know from L.A."

"Didn't you want to reconnect with your friends?" she asked.

"Those people wouldn't know how to be a friend if their lives depended on it. They're too self-centered, too shallow." He sat back in his chair. "You probably won't believe this, and I wouldn't blame you if you didn't, considering my track record. But I've been tired of the party crowd for quite some time. I just didn't realize it."

"That is pretty hard to believe," she said, tamping down a tiny bubble of hope.

Sitting forward, he reached out to take her hands in his. "Honey, I'm not going to pretend that I've been a saint since you and I were together in Los Angeles. But I can tell you that after you left, I realized that something was different about me. I suddenly felt like I wanted more out of life than being part of that scene."

"So you're telling me that I caused you to have some grand revelation about yourself?" she snorted.

He laughed. "I'm a little more thickheaded than that." His expression turned serious as he stared down at their entwined hands, then looked up to capture her gaze with his. "It's not an easy thing for me to admit, but all of my adult life I've been afraid to risk my heart, afraid to love. Deep down I was afraid I'd turn out to disappoint a woman the way my father had my mother. So I ran from it. I went out to clubs and dated more than my share of women to keep from becoming too involved."

Was he telling her he was incapable of loving?

Without warning, he reached over to lift her onto his lap. "But then I met you and all that changed."

"In what way?" It felt so wonderful to be in his arms, but she couldn't let herself believe that everything was going to work out between them. When she tried to get to her feet, to escape the temptation he posed, he tightened his arms around her.

"I couldn't forget your laughter, your smile. I couldn't forget you." He nuzzled her hair with his cheek. "I found myself lying in bed at night regretting that I hadn't learned your last name, where you were from and how I could keep in touch with you. And that's something that had never happened to me before."

"Never?" She had a hard time believing that he'd been able to forget every other woman he'd ever gone out with, but her.

"It's the truth, honey." He kissed her cheek. "I never thought I'd ever say this to a woman, but I think

I've loved you ever since I spotted you standing there at that horse auction."

Tears welled up in her eyes as the hope within her burst free and spread throughout her being. "You love me?"

"With all of my heart, Heather." He cupped her cheek with his palm. "And I'm tired of running, honey. If you can find it in your heart to forgive me for being so thick-headed, I want it all. You, marriage, brothers and sisters for Mandy. I even want the minivan filled with car seats and clumps of dog hair."

"Are you sure?" she asked cautiously.

"I've never been more certain of anything in my entire life." His smile caused her heart to skip a beat. "I love you, Heather McGwire. Will you marry me?"

"Oh, Jake, I love you, too." The tears spilled down her cheeks. "But—"

"That's all I need to hear," he said, capturing her mouth with his.

Tracing her lips with his tongue, he deepened the kiss and she knew she had to take the chance. She loved being held by him, kissed by him. And knowing that he wanted to spend a lifetime showing her how much he cared for her caused her heart to swell with more love than she'd ever thought possible.

When he finally broke the kiss, he leaned back to gaze at her and the love she saw in his eyes stole her breath. "There's something else we need to talk about," he said, smiling.

"What would that be?"

"Where we're going to live."

She worried her lower lip for a moment. She'd never imagined herself living anywhere but in the heart of Kentucky's horse-racing country. But as long as she, Mandy and Jake were together, she could live anywhere.

"I've never lived in a huge city." She took a deep breath. "But they have horses in California, too."

Giving her a smile that made her feel warm all over, he shook his head. "Don't get me wrong, I love California. It's one of the most beautiful places on earth. But I think I'd like to live right here."

"Really? Why?" She couldn't have been more surprised. "You told Hunter you were looking for a house in Malibu."

"That will be our vacation home. I want you to be able to continue making a name for yourself in the racing industry," he said. "You have a real knack for choosing bloodlines and producing champions. I want you to have the opportunity to build your reputation as the best in the business."

"I could do that in California."

He nodded. "That's true. But you've already made Hickory Hills a force to reckon with. Why not continue to build it into a racing empire?"

Loving him more with each passing second, she

laid her head on his shoulder. "What about your law office? It's in Los Angeles and quite successful. Are you sure you want to give all of that up?"

"Honey, I can practice law anywhere." He shrugged. "But to tell you the truth, I'm tired of helping people end their marriages." He paused a moment. "I think I'd like to give being a gentleman farmer a try and help my wife raise her champion thoroughbreds." He laughed. "Besides, having me around all of the time is going to save you and Clara a lot of grief."

She sat up to stare at him. "I don't understand."

"Mandy can practice her food-fighting skills on me, instead of you." He smiled. "And Daily's a good kid, but he's a lot like I was at that age."

"Heaven help us," Heather said, rolling her eyes.

His low chuckle sent a shiver coursing through her. "No kidding. I think Clara is going to have her hands full when he gets a little older and could use the help."

"I know she'll appreciate it."

Content with being in each other's arms, they remained silent for some time before he spoke again. "You never did give me an answer, honey."

"About getting married?"

He nodded. "You said you love me, but you haven't officially accepted my proposal. Will you marry me, Heather McGwire?"

"Yes."

"How soon?" His grin was bright enough to light a small city. "We've already wasted a year being apart and I'd like to make you mine as soon as possible."

Before she could tell him that she wanted that, too, the sound of the front door opening and several people entering the house intruded.

"It appears that your family has made it back from the victory party."

"Good." He set her on her feet, then rose to take her by the hand. "Let's go share our news with them."

When they walked out of the study arm in arm, everyone fell silent and turned to look at them expectantly.

His eyes never leaving hers, he announced, "I've asked Heather to marry me and she said yes."

Apparently shocked by the news, silence reigned, then everyone seemed to start talking at once.

"I'm so happy for you both," Arielle said, rushing over to give both of them a hug.

Luke laughed. "I told you so, Jake."

"Have you set a date?" Hunter wanted to know.

Smiling, Heather shook her head. "We haven't gotten that far."

Jake kissed the top of her head. "It can't be soon enough for me. If I had my way, we'd be standing in front of a minister right now."

"Me, too," Heather said, gazing up at the only man she'd ever love.

"Do you mean that?" Alyssa asked, stepping forward.

When they both nodded, Heather watched the women exchange a brief look a moment before Arielle spoke up, "We can do this, girls."

"Absolutely," Callie agreed. "Would tomorrow evening work for both of you?"

"Yes, but we can't possibly get ready in time," Heather said, disappointed. "Tomorrow is Sunday. We can't even get a marriage license until Monday."

"Don't underestimate this bunch," Haley said, laughing.

"Let's make a list." Cheyenne reached into her purse for a notepad and pen. "Nick, go get Emerald and Luther. We're going to need their help with this."

"Yes, ma'am," Nick said, his grin wide as he left the house.

When he returned with the elderly pair, Emerald breezed into the room in her satin and chiffon robe to hug Jake and Heather. "This is wonderful. I can't tell you how happy I am for you." Then, before Heather's eyes, the woman turned from a doting grandmother into a decisive, corporate giant on a mission. "Luther, find out who we know in the Louisville city government and get them to open the clerk's office first thing tomorrow morning so the kids can get their license."

Distinguished-looking even in his slippers and

robe, the older gentleman gave a stiff nod. "Consider it done, madam."

Turning back to the group, Emerald continued, "Caleb, Hunter and Nick, call your nannies and baby-sitters and tell them my corporate jet will pick them and the children up by noon tomorrow. I want the entire family to be here for this. Luke, you and Zach are assigned to helping the girls with whatever they need to pull all of this together."

"Wow!" Heather could understand why Emerald Larson was the highly successful businesswoman she was. Seeing her in action was like watching a battlefield general direct his troops.

"Heather, dear, would you prefer the ceremony be performed here or do you have somewhere else in mind?" Emerald asked, smiling.

There was no question in Heather's mind. "Right here."

"Excellent. Indoors or outside?"

"I've always dreamed of coming down that stair-case to meet my groom at the bottom of the steps," Heather answered, pointing toward the sweeping structure.

Jake gave her a tender smile. "And I'll be there waiting for you."

"Another excellent choice," Emerald approved. Turning to Heather's soon-to-be sisters-in-law, the woman grinned. "Divide up the list and get started first thing in the morning, girls. We have a wedding to get ready for tomorrow evening."

When Jake walked out of the master suite the next evening, Luke was waiting for him. "Are you ready to take the plunge?"

"I never thought I'd ever hear myself say this, but it can't be too soon," Jake admitted as they descended the stairs.

Taking his place at the bottom of the steps, he looked around. He'd never loved or appreciated his family more. They'd all worked hard to pull a wedding together on the spur of the moment and everything was picture-perfect. Heather was going to love it.

When the string quartet began to play, Jake's attention was drawn to the top of the stairs and the sight of his bride robbed him of breath. Heather was absolutely stunning. Her golden brown hair lay in soft curls around her bare shoulders and the white lace and antique satin wedding gown emphasized her enticing figure. But it was her radiant smile that he knew he'd never forget as long as he lived.

As she came down the circular staircase, he heard the baby start fussing, and walking over to Clara, took Mandy from her. Then, with his daughter in one arm, he extended his other to her beautiful mother and together they walked over to stand in front of the minister to exchange their vows and become the family he wanted with all of his heart and soul.

"Oh, Luther, I was so afraid this day might never happen," Emerald said as she dabbed her eyes with her linen handkerchief. "I was worried that Jake would turn out to be like his father and remain an irresponsible philanderer for the rest of his life."

"There was that possibility, madam," Luther agreed, nodding.

As she watched the minister pronounce Jake and Heather husband and wife, Emerald couldn't help but feel a bit sad. The investigative team she'd hired to find all of her grandchildren had concluded their search and they'd reported back that there were no more heirs to be found. Her family was finally complete.

When the group gathered in the foyer for pictures, Emerald motioned for Luther to join her. "You need to be in the picture, too, Luther. You've been instrumental in helping me find my heirs."

"It was my pleasure, madam," he said, walking over to stand at her side.

"You know, I'm going to miss helping my grandchildren find their soul mates," she whispered wistfully as the photographer tried to get the children to stand still for the picture.

"You've done a fine job with that task, madam,"

Luther said, keeping his voice low as he patted her hand. "They've all made good matches."

"After all of the unhappiness that my son caused, I'm pleased that we were able to make everything right and give them all their rightful place in Emerald, Inc." Clasping his hand with hers, she gave it a little squeeze. "Now, I can concentrate on trying to find my own bliss."

He squeezed her hand back. "I don't think you'll have far to look, madam," he said gruffly.

Turning, she gave him a happy smile. "Neither do I, Luther. Neither do I."

# Epilogue

*One year later*

"Do any of you have the slightest idea why we've been summoned to Wichita?" Jake looked at his brothers and brother-in-law expectantly as they sat in the family room at Emerald's Wichita mansion. When they all shook their heads, he shrugged. "Me neither."

"All she told me was our presence was mandatory," Luke said, setting the baby bottle down and shifting his six-month-old son to his shoulder to be burped.

"Yeah, I told her I had plans to go to a cattle auction in Denver and she told me to cancel it," Nick added.

"Arielle has become pretty close to Emerald," Hunter said, looking thoughtful. "Does she know anything, Zach?"

"If she does, she didn't tell me," he said, glancing over to check on his eight-month-old twin boys sleeping peacefully in their baby carriers beside his chair.

"When are she and our wives supposed to return from their shopping trip?" Caleb asked. "All of the kids will be waking up from their naps pretty soon and it'll turn into a three-ring circus again."

Hunter grinned. "Yeah, with ten kids between us, it does get a little hairy sometimes."

"This time next year, there'll be eleven," Jake said proudly. "We just found out Heather is pregnant."

"Make that an even dozen," Nick said, laughing. "Cheyenne is pregnant again, too."

"More like a baker's dozen," Caleb added, grinning like a fool. "Alyssa is close to entering her second trimester."

As they all congratulated each other, Emerald, Luther and their wives walked into the room. "I would imagine you're all wondering why I've asked you here for the weekend," Emerald said, smiling.

"It's crossed our minds a time or two," Luke said dryly.

When Heather walked over to sit on the arm of the chair beside him, Jake put his arm around her waist and gazed up at her. He couldn't believe how happy he'd been in the past year. Marrying her was the best thing he'd ever done. He loved her more with each passing day.

"I have a couple of announcements to make that will have a direct impact on all of you," she said, seating herself in an empty armchair.

"You have our attention," Jake said, watching Luther move to stand beside Emerald. Something was definitely up. Normally as stiff as a board, Jake had never seen the old gent look so relaxed.

"I'm retiring," Emerald said without preamble.

Jake was certain he could have heard a pin drop in the suddenly silent room. The first to find his voice, he asked, "When?"

"Next month." She paused to let the information sink in, then added, "And I'm appointing all of you to the Emerald, Inc. board of directors. I'll maintain ten percent of my stock, but the other ninety percent will be divided equally between my six grandchildren."

"Are you sure you want to do this?" Arielle asked, clearly concerned. "You started out with a home business fifty years ago and built Emerald, Inc. into a corporate empire. It's been your life."

Emerald smiled serenely. "I'm getting ready to enter a new chapter in my life."

"What are you up to this time?" Hunter asked, grinning.

Jake watched her glance at Luther and for the first time since he met the older man, Luther grinned.

"Your grandmother is going to do me the honor of becoming my bride," Luther said, placing his hand on her shoulder.

"We'll be getting married right after we both retire," Emerald said, placing her hand on Luther's. "Then we intend to take an extended honeymoon and travel the world. So I'm counting on all of you to see that Emerald, Inc. remains solid and the gold standard for corporate excellence."

After everyone expressed their surprise and promised not to let their grandmother down, Jake spoke up. "I think I speak for all of us when I say we wish you every happiness. If not for you and Luther, I might never have found Heather and Mandy."

Each of his siblings agreed that if not for Emerald and her matchmaking they might not have found their spouses and true happiness.

"Is there anything we can do to help get ready for your wedding?" Haley asked.

Jake didn't think he'd ever seen a brighter smile on his grandmother's face. "As a matter of fact, there is, dear. You all did such a wonderful job with Jake and Heather's wedding that Luther and I were wondering if you'd all like to plan ours."

"I think that's our cue to retire to the media room, boys," Hunter said, rising to his feet. "The Astros are playing the Cardinals this afternoon."

"If you don't mind, I'd quite like to join you," Luther said, surprising all of them. He kissed Emerald's cheek. "If you'll excuse me, my dear. I think

I'll attempt to 'bond,' as the younger generation are so fond of saying, with my future grandsons."

"There just might be hope for you yet, Luther," Jake said, standing to shake the older man's hand.

To his surprise, Luther actually winked. "I have twenty that says the Cardinals win. Anyone want to place a little wager?"

As Emerald watched her grandsons and the man who had stood by her side for over forty years leave to watch the ball game together, she smiled contentedly. In her day, children born out of wedlock had been considered illegitimate and in some cases went unclaimed by their families. But she'd never considered her grandchildren illegitimate. She'd searched high and low to find them and now her life was filled with more happiness than she'd ever thought possible.

She'd done everything in her power to help each one of them discover their own happiness, and to her immense satisfaction they had.

\* \* \* \* \*

Sadie jolted when Rick came up behind her. As hot
as the July sun felt on her skin, his nearness made her
temperature inch up just that much higher. There had
never been another man in her life who had affected
her the way Rick Pruitt did. Not even her ex-husband-
the-lying-cheating-weasel.

She took a breath, steadied herself, then looked up
at him, trying not to fall into those dark brown eyes.
It wasn't easy. He was tall and muscular and even in
his jeans and T-shirt, Rick looked like a man used
to giving orders and having them obeyed.

He was the quintessential Texas man. A wealthy
rancher in his own right. Add the Marine Corps to
that and you had an impossible-to-resist combination,
as the quickening heat in her body could testify.

She'd always had a reputation for being prim and
proper. The perfect Price heiress. Always doing
and saying the proper thing. But that, she assured

herself, was in another life. Just remembering the night she'd shared with Rick three years ago had her body stirring to life.

"Can you come in for a minute? There's something you need to see."

"Okay." He sounded intrigued but confused.

He wouldn't be for long.

She headed for the front door, let herself in and almost sighed with relief as the blissfully cool air-conditioned room welcomed her. A graying blonde woman in her fifties hurried over to her. "Miss Sadie, everything's fine upstairs. They're sleeping like angels."

"Thanks, Hannah," she said with a smile, not bothering to look back at Rick now. It was too late to back out. Her time had come. "I'll just go up and check on them."

The housekeeper gave Rick a long look, shifted her gaze to Sadie and smiled. "I'll be in the kitchen if you need anything."

Rick pulled his hat off and waited until Hannah was gone before he spoke. "Who's asleep? What's this about?"

"You'll see." She still didn't look at him, just walked across the marble floor toward the wide, sweeping staircase. "Come on upstairs."

She slid one hand across the polished walnut banister as she climbed the steps. Her heart was racing and a swarm of butterflies were taking flight in the pit of her stomach.

"What's going on, Sadie? In town, you said we had to talk. Then you say I've got to see something." He stepped around her when they reached the second-floor landing and blocked her way until she looked up at him. "Talk to me."

"I will," she promised, finally staring up into his eyes, reading his frustration easily. "As soon as I show you something."

"All right," he told her, "but I never did care for surprises."

The thick, patterned floor runner muffled their footsteps as they walked down the long hallway. Every step was more difficult than the last for her. But finally, she came to the last door on the left. She took a breath, turned the knob and opened it to a sunlit room.

Inside were two beds, two dressers, two toy boxes. And sitting on the floor, clearly not sleeping like angels, were her twin daughters.

*Rick's* twin daughters.

The girls looked up. Their brown eyes went wide and bright and they smiled as they spotted their mother. Sadie dropped to her knees to swoop them into her arms. With her girls held tightly to her, she turned her gaze on a stupefied Rick and whispered, "Surprise."

\* \* \* \* \*

USA TODAY *bestselling author Maureen Child*
*kicks off the brand-new miniseries,*
TEXAS CATTLEMAN'S CLUB: THE
SHOWDOWN
*They are rich and powerful, hot and wild. For*
*these Texans, it's showdown time!*
with
*ONE NIGHT, TWO HEIRS*
*Available July 2011!*

*If you liked this preview, don't miss a single*
*installment of this passionate new miniseries!*
*Available July to December 2011*
*THE REBEL TYCOON RETURNS*
*by* USA TODAY *bestselling author*
*Katherine Garbera*

*AN AFTER-HOURS AFFAIR*
*by* USA TODAY *bestselling author*
*Barbara Dunlop*

*MILLIONAIRE PLAYBOY,*
*MAVERICK HEIRESS*
*by Robyn Grady*

*TEMPTATION*
*by* NEW YORK TIMES *and*
USA TODAY *bestselling author Brenda Jackson*

*IN BED WITH THE OPPOSITION*
*by* USA TODAY *bestselling author*
*Kathie DeNosky*

# Harlequin® *Desire*

ALWAYS POWERFUL, PASSIONATE AND PROVOCATIVE.

**Save $1.00**
on the purchase of
ONE NIGHT, TWO HEIRS
by MAUREEN CHILD
or any other
Harlequin Desire® title.

*On Sale July 2011*

- - - - - - - - - - - - - - - - - - - - - - - - - - - - - - - - ✂

**SAVE $1.00** on the purchase of *One Night, Two Heirs* by Maureen Child or any other Harlequin Desire® title.

Coupon expires December 31, 2011. Redeemable at participating retail outlets in the U.S. and Canada only. Limit one coupon per customer.

52609930

5 65373 00076 2   (8100)0 11754

HDBAPCOUP11

# Spread the joy of love and romance!

*The Billionaire's Unexpected Heir* is a passionate story of second chances as billionaire Jake Garnier reconnects with the one woman he's never stopped thinking about, and discovers she has a secret that will change his life forever. This is a story you can share with friends, family, book club members or anyone you think would enjoy a romantic read!

## Here are some ideas for sharing books:

◆ Give to your sister, daughter, granddaughter, mother, friends or coworkers
◆ Host your own book club
◆ Share the books with members of your church group, community group or PTA
◆ Share them at your community center, retirement home or hospital and brighten someone's day

### OR

◆ Leave them for others to enjoy on an airplane, in a coffee shop, at the Laundromat, doctor's/dentist's office, hairdresser, spa or vacation spot

**Please tell us about your experience reading and sharing these books at**

# www.tellharlequin.com.

**Harlequin**®

A *Romance* FOR EVERY MOOD™

---

Experience the variety
of romances that
Harlequin has to offer...

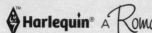 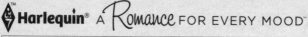

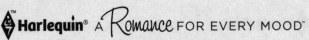

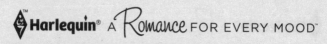

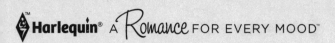

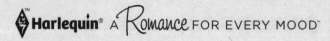